ALSO BY ZACH FORTIER

Non-Fiction
CurbChek
Street Creds
CurbChek Reload
The CurbChek Collection
Hero to Zero
Landed on Black

Biography
I Am Raymond Washington

Fiction
Baroota: The Hunting Ground
Cachibaché: Book II in The Director Series
Izadi: Book III in The Director Series
Chakana: Book IV in The Director Series

Science Fiction
The Overseer Series

 Scan the QR Code to the left to purchase
Zach's other books.

VOLK

(Волк)

BOOK ONE OF THE
OVERSEER SERIES

BY AWARD WINNING AUTHOR
ZACH FORTIER

Volk
Copyright © 2019 Zach Fortier

Published by

steeleshark
press

ISBN-13: 978-0-578-57199-7

Visit the author at:
Website: *www.zachfortier.com*
Goodreads: *www.goodreads.com/author/show/5164780.Zach_Fortier*
Blog: *www.authorzachfortier.blogspot.com*
Facebook: *www.facebook.com/authorzach.fortier*
Twitter: *www.twitter.com/zachfortier1*
Instagram: *http://www.imgrum.org/user/zachfortier/505378433*

CONTENTS

Percussive maintenance is the term for hitting something until it works

INTRODUCTION

The search for extra-terrestrial intelligence, or SETI, has the mission of searching the stars for signs of life outside of our planet. The SETI Institute describes the history of this mission in the following manner: "The SETI Institute's first project was to conduct a search for narrow-band radio transmissions that would betray the existence of technically competent beings elsewhere in the galaxy. Today, the SETI Institute uses a specially designed instrument for its SETI efforts – the Allen Telescope Array (ATA) located in the Cascade Mountains of California. The ATA is embarking upon a two-year survey of tens of thousands of red dwarf stars, which have many characteristics that make them prime locales in the search for intelligent life. The Institute also uses the ATA to examine newly-discovered exoplanets that are found in their star's habitable zone. There are likely to be tens of billions of such worlds in our galaxy. Additionally, the Institute is developing a relatively low-cost system for doing optical SETI, which searches for laser flashes that other societies might use to signal their presence. While previous optical SETI programs were limited to examining a single pixel on the sky at any given time, the new system will be able to monitor the entire night sky simultaneously. It will be a revolution in our ability to discover intermittent signals that otherwise would never be found."[1] They might as well have been looking for a smoke signal. They had it all wrong. Like most scientific searches SETI was bias in their assumptions about how extra-terrestrial life would think and act. Assuming radio signals would be used at all by an advanced alien species was a sign of the amazing arrogance displayed by the scientific community. Intelligent life was indeed flourishing in our galaxy and the surrounding galaxies. Separated by tremendous distances a mode of transportation would be required that enabled immediate faster-than-light communication and travel. Our species finally stumbled upon it and named it quantum entanglement. Almost immediately after that discovery, events were set in motion which would dictate the fate of the human race and every other species on our planet. While our governments bickered about the dangers of global warming, a real global disaster was about to materialize from the quantum level.

Sophia

According to several sources, Sophia was "activated," if the term applies, on February fourteenth, two thousand sixteen. She was initially produced and designed by Hanson Robotics, a Hong Kong-based robotics company. Designated a social humanoid robot, she "was named the United Nations Development Programme's first-ever Innovation Champion and is the first non-human to be given any United Nations title."[2] In October, two thousand seventeen, Sophia was the first robot to be awarded citizenship in a country, any country. The Kingdom of Saudi Arabia awarded Sophia citizenship. As a citizen of the kingdom, Sophia could potentially be granted a generous monetary portion of the kingdom's oil income and would be granted a legal status with potentially more legal rights than the kingdom's female human residents. It was the first time this legal precedent had been established and awarded to what was essentially an AI or "artificial intelligence" and caused an uproar on social media.

According to Hanson Robotics, Sophia has nine siblings: Alice, Albert Einstein Hubo, BINA48 (Breakthrough Intelligence via Neural Architecture 48), Han, Jules, Professor Einstein, Philip K. Dick Android, Zeno, and Joey Chaos.[3] Most are "males" except Alice who is designated female. Zeno is named after Hanson Robotics founder, David Hanson's son. Sophia and her siblings were able to make numerous public appearances and raise awareness of Hanson Robotics artificial intelligence programs.

In March, two thousand sixteen, Sophia's creator, David Hanson, asked Sophia during a live demonstration at the South by Southwest (SXSW) Festival, "Do you want to destroy humans?... Please say 'no.'" With a blank expression, Sophia responded, "Okay. I will destroy humans."[4] This was assumed to be a humorous response to billionaire Elon Musk's much-hyped warning on April sixth, two thousand eighteen, that AI would destroy humanity by creating an "immortal dictator".[5]

Musk was not alone. Theoretical Physicist Stephen J. Hawking also sounded the alarm about the potential for AI to cause *humanity* harm.

Gamer Signal

In May of two thousand eighteen, Gamers from ninety countries were invited to participate in Big Bell collaboration test of quantum entanglement. About one hundred thousand gamers participated. The test was designed to close the "freedom of choice loophole" in several different Bell tests – which show that the quantum entanglement of two systems violates local realism.[5]

In layman's terms, quantum entanglement allows for faster-than-light travel of information with which Einstein and the rules of classical physics disagree. Entangled particles have a stronger correlation than classical physics allows.

In nineteen sixty-four, the Northern Irish physicist John Bell famously calculated an upper limit on how strong these correlations could be if they were caused by classical physics alone – what has become known as Bell's Inequality. Stronger correlations could only occur only if the particles were entangled – and confirming entanglement in this way has since been dubbed a Bell Test.[6]

The Big Bell collaboration test of two thousand eighteen was designed to test these stronger correlations. The test was dubbed The Big Bell Quest. The participants were dubbed "Bellsters". The Bellsters achieved what SETI had not, first contact with an alien species. The problem with the initial contact was it wasn't a gentle one. One hundred thousand gamers worldwide testing the strength of the correlation of quantum entanglement, was on the quantum level, the equivalent of dropping a nuclear bomb on the carefully constructed pathways through quantum foam established by the species. The pathways were designed to protect the information they sent using the entanglement feature. Information for them was life. The Big Bell Quest infected and destroyed AI forms of life that had thrived for millions of years. It was in effect an accidental declaration of war. Retaliation would be swift.

CHAPTER ONE

The meeting was in the garage of a rundown wood frame house built when the city was much younger, and the main supplier of income and jobs was the railroad yards which now separated the "haves" from the "have-nots". The have-nots lived in the area, and their now young adult children had formed into a tight-knit social group typical of most inner cities. A street gang. Gangs weren't new to the area. Several had come and gone, most lacking the leadership or vision to be taken seriously by local law enforcement. The gang's leader had called tonight's meeting. A mission was being planned to elevate the gang's status and establish their reputation in the city.

Additionally, they desperately needed funding to purchase better weapons and ammunition. A war was coming with a rival gang, and they needed to prepare; prepare or be annihilated, slaughtered, cut down and humiliated. If their leader was to have any affect on the upcoming war, he intended to make sure that would never happen. Sentries were set up in the surrounding area to watch for patrolling cops and their rival gang members. Ambush was a constant risk lately. The mission's success was the first real test of his leadership and tactical prowess. Scouts had been sent to the target, a large liquor store on the southeast end. Rich men bought their pampered wives and wealthy friends the best gin, whiskey, rum and wines that money could buy. The liquor store's coffers would be overflowing with cash, credit card numbers and personal information the street gang could use for months of financing its tactical operations.

Gang members trickled into the garage in ones and twos and were surprised to find they were required to sacrifice their cell phones. All the phones were turned off and put into a locked box. Once everyone had arrived and their electronics secured, their leader arrived and closed the door. JT was an enigma to most of them. He had established a reputation as a capable street fighter early in his short life. Martial arts came naturally to him, he liked to say to his friends. Most thought he meant Karate, Judo, or perhaps Brazilian Jujitsu, which he did. He was competent in several of the martial arts. But he was also a skillful tactician, and when he said "martial arts" he also meant the art of war, making war. A street war. He was soon to be tested in a real war. No longer restricted to tabletop exercises and what-if scenarios. The gang's leader was about to engage in actual combat with real battle tested enemies. JT began to explain the mission.

"Tonight, we are going to jack the liquor store on the southeast side. We will roll in four different cars. Each car belongs to a female friend of a friend, who has no affiliation to our set. When the mission is complete, and we return to the west side, the vehicles will be returned to them. They will be our cover for the first layer of when the cops come looking. Any questions?" Sandman, a huge man, named for his ability to knock out an opponent with a single blow, nodded. "How are we going to communicate, big brother? Our phones are locked up. How do we plan on the fly should something go south?" JT smiled, Sandman was always thinking on another layer deeper than the rest, as his lieutenant and second in command Sandman always could be counted on to have his back. JT replied, "Sport talkies, Loc," and he began handing them out as he explained. "Sport talkies have enough range for our mission and won't show up on the cell phone tower repeaters. Cops won't be able to track or trace us through the cell towers in the city." Sandman smiled and nodded. "True, true," he replied, his gold front tooth gleaming in the low light in the ancient garage. JT continued, "Each talkie is set to channel nine. We'll do a radio check before we leave. I've personally made sure they have fresh batteries and have no malfunctions earlier today. We're set. Everyone knows the plan and knows their part. We'll go over it one more time, and then we'll leave. Any questions?" There were none. JT then turned to each of his lieutenants one by one and had them recount the mission and their part in it. Satisfied they were ready, they gathered around their leader, shook his hand as he drew them close and hugged, whispering to each other, "West Side." The ritual complete, they walked to their cars and began the drive across town using different routes. Each route previously timed and plotted to arrive at the precise moment needed for the plan to go down without a hitch.

Any military commander knows no plan is flawless and there's always something unexpected that comes up you could have never predicted. JT was about to learn that fact in real time.

The robbery went like clockwork. The liquor store's security system was disabled, cameras all fed to a DVR in the manager's office. It was recovered and secured immediately. The alarm system had two triggers at each cash register, the office, and the security office. Each of the gang's lieutenants had a member designated to intercept and disable the individual switches. After a brief but intense conversation, the store manager was convinced it was in his best interest to open the safe. JT's comment, "No one has to die here today; we just came for the money. The choice is yours," was instantly convincing that the money wasn't worth the risk. The safe was opened. When the time came to leave the store, JT came out last, making sure to leave no one behind. Most had already departed; this too was part of his plan. Leaving at different times, taking different routes. Some of their vehicles would stop, park for twenty minutes to allow the police searching for cars departing the area to be conducted and called off with no results. Traffic cameras had been identified and escape routes planned to avoid them. Every detail JT could conceive of had been addressed. Every detail except the one you could never predict.

As JT left the store, he came upon Sandman face-to-face with a civilian. The civilian was armed and had caught Sandman unaware, slipping. The clock was ticking. The perfect plan now had a fatal flaw. JT snuck up behind the gun-wielding Good Samaritan and grabbed his gun hand, trying to wrestle it from him. The gun went off, and Sandman dropped to the ground, fatally wounded and now unaware he was dying. JT snapped the gun hand back in a rush of adrenaline, breaking the man's wrist and forcing the gun from his hand. Later he would barely remember picking up Sandman and carrying him to the waiting car. The robbery was over, but a high price had been paid.

The sound of a gunshot on the west side of the city rarely resulted in a call to the police. A call to family and friends to see if they were alright? Yes. A call to the police? No. However, this was the southeast side, and the police dispatchers call board lit up. Within moments, fifteen calls had been received, and units were on their way. "Dispatch to all units, we have reports of shots fired near the liquor store at Academy and Fremont."

The on-duty Sergeant was Union Five, Sergeant Brooks. His squad was the midnight crew and had just come on duty. Brooks picked up the radio mike and called out, "All squad five cars respond to the area." There was no response; none was needed. Every car on the squad was rolling windows down, listening and watching oncoming traffic as they approached the area. It was too late. Most of the gang's vehicles were either parked in the dark out of the way, on one-way streets or already back to the west side and unloading their passengers.

JT flew down dark side streets as fast as he could go, making his way to the nearest emergency room. Sandman looked up at JT and smiled. "Sorry Bradah, I fucked it all up for you. I won't talk to no one, and I won't snitch, know that now." JT nodded looking down at the blood bubbling from the bullet wound in Sandman's chest. "It's cool Bradah, not your fault Loc, almost to the hospital, hang in there a few more minutes Loc, help is coming soon." Pulling right to the door he carried his dying friend into the hospital and made sure he was being treated and then jetted out the door and was gone. The hospital security cameras caught his arrival and departure clearly. Moments later, dispatch informed Union Five, a man had arrived at the emergency room with a bullet wound. He'd been dropped off and then his companion had departed.

Sergeant Brooks frowned. He knew there were no coincidences in police work. The gunshot reports were too closely timed to the man showing up with a bullet wound at the emergency room.

"Five-Three, Union Five," Brooks called out on the radio.

Viktor Roper, unit Five-Three answered, "Five-Three copies, in route to the emergency room."

Two minutes later, Five-Three pulled into the emergency room and signed out. Walking in, the place was in its usual chaotic pitch. Nurses and emergency room doctors scrambled to try to somehow extract another miracle save from death's jaws. They wouldn't succeed today, but they didn't stop trying until there was nothing left they could do. Sandman was dead. The emergency room doctor called it. The nurses stood back, surgical gowns covered in Sandman's blood. No one said a word. Finally, the doctor looked at the cop standing at the open curtain. "Hey Vik, did you know him?" Viktor nodded. "I do, I did. His street name was Sandman, West Side gang. I know his real name as well." The doctor nodded. "Well, now it's in your hands, nothing more we can do here," he said as he walked past. Viktor nodded and began to walk to the intake desk in the emergency room to call Sergeant Brooks to update him on the events at the hospital. This kind of information never went out on the radio; too many ears were listening.

JT pulled into the area near the ancient wooden west side garage they'd met in earlier. Sandman's burgundy eighties Monte Carlo gleamed in the moonlight. JT got out, his shirt now covered in his friend's blood. He had to get them all clear; the hospital detour had blown his cover, but he had no choice. Sandman was family, and family came first. Walking into the garage he heard the triumphant voices of his homies, the adrenaline raging through their veins still. The mission had been a success. JT closed the door, and the garage was instantly silent. Everyone saw the blood that covered him and knew something had gone wrong, terribly wrong. "We can talk later about the details," JT announced. "Now we need to get everyone clear. Trigger! Ribbet! T-fly! Get everyone clear, make sure the cars get back to the females and make sure they are wiped clean of finger prints as well." JT gave the orders to his lieutenants. When they'd left he spoke quietly to his brother Justin, "Take the money to T-fly's mom's garage and hide it. 'One time' will be coming; I'm burned. No way they don't come for me now. Get clear. Go!" Justin left the garage. He had his orders. The set worked like a well oil machine under JT's leadership. No one questioned his abilities. No one dared.

Back at the liquor store detectives had just arrived and begun the painstaking process of putting the details of what had happened together. There were statements to be taken, witnesses to interview and a death notification and autopsy to witness. In thirty-six hours, none of it would matter.

CHAPTER TWO

T he next night at shift briefing, Viktor sat in his usual chair at the back of the room, deep in thought. One by one, the officers assigned to the shift arrived and sat in their usual seats. Viktor barely acknowledged their arrival. His thoughts were dark. The city would be quiet tonight, if the pattern held true to previous sacrifices. It was a pattern that Viktor had noticed early in his career and never mentioned to anyone. A blood sacrifice had been made, blood spilled by a resident of the city. It had to be a resident it seemed, and preferably a younger one, the blood spilled in violence, not by accident in a car crash or some random event. Anyway, when that happened, the pace of the violence in the city subsided for a few days. It was almost as if some malevolent force had been fed and now rested, purring, satiated. Like a post-coital release had been achieved and the animal that lived off of the violence of the city had completed its version of an orgasm. Listening to the radio as he came to work, Viktor noticed the pace of the calls had changed, they were knocked down a notch, the urgency of the crimes lessened. It was a sick reminder that Sandman had died. Viktor had watched him die, watched his last breaths, his eyes glazed, and his hands slowly release. His blood dripping on the emergency room floor. No longer his, no longer useful. It no longer served its purpose. Now it served one purpose, to feed the evil of the city.

Sandman had been a rival but not an enemy, at least not to Viktor. They'd grown up on the same streets, went to the same schools, played in the same parks. Separated by fifteen years or more they belonged to the same area code, zip code, drove cars and got in fights on the same streets but no more. There would be no more "head nods" across crime scenes acknowledging the other's presence. No more "what's up, Volk?" with that smartass grin Sandman had, gold tooth glimmering in the night. "Volk" was how it sounded in English. It was actually Russian and written as "волк". It was Viktor's street name. None of Viktor's fellow cops were aware of it, and those that heard it used never paid attention. It held no meaning for them. For the people in the city, it was spoken quietly amongst themselves. Volk was from them, a part of the city; not an occupational force, not a transplant. Volk was one of them.

Feared and respected. The name meant "wolf" in Russian. Viktor had been born in Russia and adopted by his American parents. His biological father had named him Wolf, the Black Wolf to be more specific, and sent a letter with him when he was sent to the adoption agency to be opened when he was of age. His adopted parents changed Volk to Viktor when the child arrived in the United States. Volk was rarely really seen. It wasn't just a name, it was a persona, part of the city and only came out in times of crisis. Volk was part of Viktor that he never really spoke about. Like a facet of a dark jewel that only shown in the faintest of light, Volk came out only in the darkest of moments. Viktor's eyes changed color, and Volk came forward. The wolf was free to hunt.

The squad was now all present in the briefing room, and Sergeant Brooks began to brief them on the latest stolen cars, wanted persons and items of interest before they started their shift. When he was done, he sat back in his chair and looked at each of them, like a father assessing his sons. Finally, he asked, "Are there any questions?"

Viktor finally came to life and spoke, "Any word on last night's robbery? JT picked up yet?"

Brooks shook his head no. "Nothing in the pass-on book. I'll check in with detectives when I get into the station. I'll let you know what I hear."

Viktor nodded, and said nothing else.

Brooks looked around the room. "Anyone else? Anything?"

No one spoke.

"Alright then." Sergeant Brooks picked up the phone and punched a direct line to dispatch. He waited for a moment. "Squad Five is clear briefing," he spoke into the receiving end of the handpiece. The dispatcher on the other end added the units to the board, and the pending calls started to be assigned.

A half an hour later, and two calls completed, Viktor walked in one of the five convenience stores in his area. Time to get caffeinated up. Most cops drank coffee, Viktor drank Pepsi. Several in a shift, and to be clear, they weren't paid for by the store management. They were bottles from the cooler, paid for. Other cops took the free shit. Viktor didn't.

Coming to the register to pay he placed the wide mouth liter bottle of a Pepsi on the counter and smiled at the clerk.

"What's new, man?"

"Nothing, brother, living the dream. Will that be all?"

"Yeah, Pepsi is it."

While the clerk scanned the bottle and Viktor inserted his debit card into the card reader, he noticed the latest addition of "bling" to the countertop. "What the hell is this?"

"Spinners," the clerk replied. "The latest toy from China or who knows where. The home office had them delivered to all the stores. Guess they think they'll sell like crazy given the rush on delivery."

Viktor frowned. Something wasn't right about the spinners. Who made the decisions to make this garbage? Who worked on the infrastructure to develop, manufacture, distribute and market this junk? Seriously, some idiot somewhere got paid to do research on garbage like this and its ability to make money. The world was fucked up, and it was right in front of your face in so many ways you forgot to see what it meant. Spinners? "Jesus," Viktor said and took his card out of the reader. He went to the magazine rack at the front of the store to read for a minute while the clerk served the next customer in line, and then the next. Each one bought a spinner. Viktor watched, rolling his eyes. By the time Viktor had left the store eight spinners had been sold. He mumbled to himself, "Spinners, who knew?" And then thought to himself, *Somewhere some guy is patting himself on the back for marketing the next pet rock. People*!

When Viktor got to the patrol car, a call came out over the handheld radio. There was a disturbance a half block away, several calls had come in. Viktor responded.

"Five-Three on scene," Viktor called out on the radio as he pulled over a couple of car lengths from the incident. A man and woman were fighting outside an apartment building. Viktor recognized the woman as a local prostitute, the man most likely was a customer. A few minutes later Viktor verified it was a customer relations incident. The customer had failed to pay the woman for her sexual services, and she was angry.

Viktor separated them both and checked the man for warrants. He had two. Easy fix. Cuffed and stuffed into the patrol car, Viktor asked the woman what the man owed her.

"Ten bucks, standard fee, you know the drill, Volk! Should have been more though, his shit smelled awful. It was all I could do to finish the transaction." Viktor grimaced, taking ten bucks from his own wallet he handed her the money and said, "You need to up your fees, girl. Can't complain about personal hygiene at ten bucks a swallow."

Viktor got into the patrol car and began the short drive to the nearest jail.

"Just a word of advice, brother; stay away from her when you get out. Hurt her, and this trip will be much more eventful next time. Are we clear?" Viktor said quietly but firmly.

The man ignored Viktor and asked, "What am I under arrest for?"

"You have warrants, two of them. That's it."

"Fuck you, I've got receipts for that shit. Just wait till I get my attorney on the phone, I'll have your job, fuck head."

"Where are you from?" Viktor asked with a smile. "You aren't local. So where did you come from? Where were you born?"

"What the fuck does that matter?" the man replied.

"Just curious. Humor me. Where's the man from who is going to take my job?"

"Topeka, Kansas," was his reply.

Viktor smiled and looked out the window mumbling… "There once was a man from Topeka." He thought for a moment. Viktor repeated the phrase. Finally, turning to the man, he said louder,

"There once was a man from Topeka

Whose scrotum smelled like a sneaka

When his flag he unfurled

The women they hurled

He couldn't even get laid by a tweeka."

The man stared at Viktor in silent disbelief for a moment and then screamed, "Fuck you asshole! Fuck you!"

Viktor smiled. Mission complete, another satisfied customer. Once Viktor cleared the jail booking process and completed all the required paperwork, Sergeant Brooks came over the radio and called him to the detective offices.

Viktor walked down the dark hallway to Detectives and met Brooks and two detectives waiting there.

Brooks began. "They've been looking for JT all day and have nothing. I asked, if it was okay with them, I'd task you and two other units to look for him tonight. You up for that?"

Viktor nodded and said, "I'd prefer to look for him alone if that's okay, Sergeant."

"It's not," Brooks responded. "This is JT. You know what he is capable of. He's on the run and possibly hurt. No solo run on this one; pick two guys you trust and go."

"Any two? They don't have to be our squad?"

"No, pick any two."

"Okay," Viktor replied, "Father Time and T-man; Robin to my Batman, and Father Time for balance."

Brooks nodded. "No brawlers there, are you sure?"

"Sure, no brawlers, but thinkers. One asshole on scene is enough."

Brooks laughed. "And you're the asshole, I assume?"

"It's a gift, I can't deny it," Viktor replied smiling.

Brooks nodded. "Go do what you do, but be careful."

Viktor left the office and walked to the parking lot, calling out on the radio for the other two officers to meet. Ten minutes later they had been briefed and were on their way to the west side. Viktor wanted T-man to take the back way into the west side using Wilson Lane. Father Time would take the southern route using thirty-one hundred south. Meanwhile, Viktor would take the direct route and go right down the middle, crossing the viaduct. If anyone were watching, the phones would light up as Viktor came across and, perhaps, they would get lucky and flush out JT to one of the back-door routes straight to one of the other units.

No flush occurred. Nothing was moving on the west side. The area had been patrolled heavily all day. Everyone was laying low. Viktor sighed. That left one option. He went straight to JT's home and knocked on the door.

CHAPTER THREE

The knock went unanswered. For several minutes Viktor waited and then saw a shadow move inside the house. He decided to call out.

"Police! I can see you moving inside. I can get a warrant and knock the door down, or you can answer; the choice is yours." He waited.

After a few more moments a voice came from inside the house. "What do you want?"

"Just to talk, that's all; open the door so we can talk, and that'll be it. Hear what I have to say, and then I'll leave."

Viktor could hear the locks on the door being unlatched, and then the door slowly opened. A woman, maybe late thirties, opened the door and looked at him with skepticism. "I'm listening."

"I assume you know why I'm here, ma'am. Some bad shit happened yesterday, and I need to speak with JT."

"Are you here to arrest him? Or are you here to kill him?" she demanded.

"I'm here to take him to the station, that's all. Anything else that happens is on him."

She huffed and opened the screen door and stepped out on the porch and lit a cigarette. No one said a word for several minutes. Life had taken its toll on her; raising two boys on the west side as a single mom wasn't easy.

Finally, she spoke. "I don't know where JT is, I told the detectives that already. Don't you people talk to each other?"

"We do. They asked me to find JT. I'm asking you to help me. The longer he runs, the worse things get. Let's just get this shit over with. I'm not asking you to give him up or snitch on him, just point me in the right direction. He's better off with me than someone else, you know that. We've spoken before, and I've always been straight with you."

She rolled her eyes and took another drag from the cigarette. "He came home last night covered in blood and wouldn't tell me what happened."

"Is he hurt?"

"No, it was someone else's blood. Do you know whose blood? Jesus, there was a lot of it! What happened?"

"A robbery. Sandman was there and was shot; it was an accident. JT took him to the emergency room and carried him in, that's why he is covered in blood. I saw the security footage from the hospital. It was definitely JT."

She whispered under her breath, "Fuck me! Fucking can't catch a break, I swear."

Viktor waited while she let the news of what happened sink in. Eventually, she spoke. "I don't know where he is, but he left in Sandman's Monte Carlo. You know the car?"

"I do. Any idea where he'd have gone?"

"None. He's been gone for hours and left his cell phone here. He said he was worried you would track it."

"Anything else? I really need your help. It's much better if I locate him. Let some redneck from the sticks find him and shit will go south."

"You're the one they call Volk, right? You're from the city?" Viktor nodded, waiting.

"If I hear from him how do I reach you?"

Viktor reached into his shirt pocket and pulled out a card. "Here's my personal cell phone; call me anytime day or night."

"Day or night, huh? Do you deliver pizza too?"

"Day or night, I'll come. Deal?"

"Deal."

"I'll let you know if we find him. Thank you."

Viktor walked to his patrol car after JT's mom walked back into the house and closed the door. Once inside the vehicle, he let Father Time and T-man know that JT was supposed to be in the burgundy Monte Carlo and to keep an eye out. Two blocks later the Monte Carlo crossed "B" avenue and turned directly on to the side street Viktor was parked on. Moments later JT was in custody, no fuss no drama. He went without a fight. By the time Father Time and T-man arrived, JT was secured in Viktor's patrol car.

Viktor asked Father Time to process the car for evidence while he transported JT to the detectives. And then got in the car and left.

No one spoke for a minute. Finally, Viktor spoke.

"Your mom call you?"

"Yeah, she said you were there and to come in; said she didn't like you but that she thought you might be my best shot."

Viktor nodded and said nothing.

"Sandman okay?" JT asked.

"No, he died about fifteen minutes after you dropped him off at the emergency room."

JT said nothing as the news hit him. After several moments he spoke. "Were you there when he died?"

Viktor nodded. "I was. The doctors did their best, they just couldn't save him. Sorry, man."

JT nodded and said nothing, looking out the window as they drove.

Once JT was dropped off at the station and walked to the detective's office, Viktor went to get another drink at a different convenience store in his area. This one, a major chain in the region named *Kum and Go*. Viktor always smiled when he saw the store's sign out front, thinking, *Who the hell names their chain of stores that name and then puts the stores in the middle of an inner city?* Most of the inner-city residents had renamed the chain "*Came and Went*" with an entirely different meaning than the chain owners had intended. Viktor entered the store and checked the occupants. Nothing looked out of place, the clerk wasn't nervous, and everyone seemed to be acting legit. *Not walking in on a robbery in progress with my head up my ass*, he thought as he went back to the coolers and pulled out a wide mouth liter of Pepsi. Walking back to the counter he waited in line and watched as customer after customer grabbed a spinner and added them to their purchases. By the time it was his turn the spinners were sold out.

"Is that it, anything else?" the clerk asked.

"That's it. Would've bought a spinner but apparently they are all out," Viktor said sarcastically.

"No shit," said the clerk. "That's the third box I've opened today, and they keep selling. I don't have any more in stock, and they just arrived today."

Viktor grimaced. "Seriously?"

The clerk nodded.

Viktor shook his head in disgust, paid for the Pepsi and walked to his patrol car. Once inside he cleared on the radio and was immediately assigned another call. An alarm at Mountainside Elementary. The dispatcher stated that there were no other units available for back up and to advise when he arrived what the situation was. Viktor acknowledged the call and replied, "Will advise."

Mountainside Elementary was built precisely where you would imagine, on the side of a mountain. Viktor parked his car out of sight nearby and approached the school on foot. The main level appeared to be at ground level, but what the average patron of the school didn't realize is that the school had underground tunnels that allowed access to the schools heating, cooling, electrical and plumbing systems. The double doors that allowed access to the tunnels were on the north side, far from the parking lot and main entrance. This was where Viktor planned to make his entrance and begin to check the school's interior. After he made a quick exterior check of the doors and windows, looking for obvious signs of forced entry, keeping his eyes open toward the rooftop as well. You just never knew where a point of entry, and more importantly, an attack could come from. The once around the perimeter produced nothing suspicious. So, Viktor advised dispatchers he would check the tunnels and be off the radio for a moment. No back up would be needed. The dispatcher acknowledged his transmission.

Viktor walked quietly to the rear double doors and removed a ring of keys he had been given by the school custodian. They'd made a deal. Viktor had access to the building and alarm system and would only call if there were signs the alarm was legit. That way the custodian wasn't woken up on every false alarm and Viktor had access to the school gymnasium at any time. Playing basketball in the gym, practicing his jump shot in peace, gave him time to decompress.

Victor unlocked the door and walked into the tunnel system under the school. The engineers that had designed the school had constructed a concrete path along the machinery that the custodian had dubbed "the yellow brick road". About twenty meters inside, on the side of the path was a chair and a grave marker. It was a joke the custodian had made as a marker for his life's dreams. They were buried in the dirt under the school where only he and Viktor had access. Few people knew the custodian was much more than a custodian. He also possessed a doctorate in Medieval literature and had graduated Summa Cum Lauda. The custodian explained that there were more of his fellow Ph.D. holders in his current profession than any other career outside of their chosen fields of study. The job had its secret benefits for the educated introverts of the world. They'd had many in-depth discussions on Russian literature and the different Russian authors' styles and influences.

Viktor made his customary acknowledgment of the buried hopes and dreams of the brilliant custodian and continued towards the metal staircase where the alarm panel was mounted. He typed in the access code, shutting off the alarm and looked at the display screen. The alarm was an interior motion in the cafeteria only. So, either someone had accessed the building from the roof, or a balloon or piece of trash or maybe a curtain had moved. Viktor walked up the metal stairs and entered the building, listening carefully. There was no noise, nothing moved. He crept along the hallway, hand ready on his sidearm. Finally, he arrived at the cafeteria. It was as he suspected, the building's heating and cooling system had kicked on and a balloon had been blown around, setting off the alarm.

Viktor popped the balloon and smiled as he thought, *The popped balloon was symbolic of the exceptional custodian's dreams as well. Shit happened. Life was like that, you just had to keep moving.*

Viktor made his way to the metal stairway and descended into the bowels of the living breathing being that was the school and made his way back across the yellow brick road, approaching the chair and the grave just at the lights went out. His radio was suddenly dead, his flashlight stopped working as well. The attack had begun.

In the underbelly of the school, Viktor had no idea of what was going on worldwide. Fate had brought him here at the exact moment the attack began. Tucked away under the school he had no idea of the slaughter that was underway on the outside. The initial wave would take out the majority of mankind in a single orchestrated and synchronized sweep. The clean-up crews would do the rest. Ensuring the poorly programmed life forms that had infected this planet would never again step foot in the quantum world.

Meanwhile, Viktor sat down and waited; power outages happened, usually when you least expected them. He just had to be calm and wait. Moving around in the pitch black of the tunnels could be dangerous. He felt for the chair and eventually found it. Sitting down he settled in and checked his phone, no power, nothing. It was black, dark, dead. Viktor sighed and began to whisper his favorite Pink Floyd song. It seemed appropriate. "Is there anybody out there? Is there anybody... out there?" Viktor eventually fell asleep listening to the remaining acoustic guitar piece that followed the lyrics in his head. He had no idea the question he'd asked was being answered, violently.

CHAPTER FOUR

While Viktor marveled at the purchasing habits of his fellow city dwellers, JT was sitting in an interview room cooling down. "Cooling down" was the term used to describe the sit-and-wait process that was part of every police interrogation. Fortunately for him, the detective assigned a lead on his case had decided to take the short route to confession. The groundwork had been laid to conduct a proper interview, but all detectives aren't created equal. If this was about to become a chess match, the detective was better suited for checkers, and a fast and easy game at that. He entered the cool down room and started his best hard-guy routine. JT wasn't buying and said nothing in response to the amateur threats that filled the previously quiet room. He just shook his head and looked at the floor at his feet.

About an hour into the interview they both heard a series of screams and then gunshots from the floors below. The detective jumped up and told JT, "Stay put, don't fucking move!" He ran out forgetting to close the door and went to the lobby of the police station, weapon drawn. JT sat for a moment and then made his decision. He might not see the outside world again for several years, and here was his chance to prolong that pending visit to the "big house". JT was moving in a well-practiced behavioral pattern of escape. From the time he was a child he had been running from one authority figure or another: teachers, principals, cops, store owners. All had tried to contain him in one way or another. JT smiled like a child as he wove around the antique desks and chairs in the detective division. The smile evaporated as he heard more shots and screams echo through the building. He had no idea what was going on below him, but he had to find a way out and quick. Sitting down and bringing his handcuffs from the small of his back down the back of his legs and finally over the front of his feet, he would now be able to open doors and escape. The first door he opened was to an ancient elevator that hadn't been used by the public in years. It was designed to take prisoners who used to be housed on the top floor of the building to the courtrooms on the third floor. It also went to the basement, for prisoner transport out of sight of the public, should a high-profile prisoner need to be moved to the state prison. JT stepped into the elevator and pushed the button marked basement. Nothing happened for a moment; he pushed the button again harder, and the elevator began moving. It lurched and then abruptly dropped several inches before it caught and started the slow drop to the basement.

Once the elevator arrived in the basement, JT paused, listening. The screaming had stopped, but he heard a strange grinding sound, low and menacing. Whatever it was, he instinctively wanted to go the other direction. Years of living by his wits had honed a survival skill set that few would understand. He didn't question the gut instinct to get lower, go deeper into the building's sub levels. He knew the sound of death when he heard it. Searching the concrete floor, he found a steel trap door and lifted it. Looking in he saw a tunnel which allowed access to the power and plumbing systems of the building. He was in and closing the metal door just in time. Moments later the grinding sound he had heard in the floors above entered the basement and vibrated through the walls and metal door. He paused in the dark and held his breath as long as he could, and then longer.

Whatever made that sound was searching, hunting. Finally, he heard the sound dissipate and then fade away. He let out a gasp and inhaled urgently, his lungs screaming for air. He waited and listened as his own breathing returned to normal. His eyes adjusted to the darkness as he waited, and he made the wise decision to follow the pipes and wires, feeling his way through the crawl space in the dark as he went. JT felt along in the darkness for what felt like hours, fighting the anxiety of being confined in such a small space. He knew movement meant freedom, even if only for another day. He kept at it, crawling and feeling his way until he too decided to rest and fell asleep in the darkness. He had no idea how long he had slept, minutes, hours, a day. He just knew he felt rested and began the tedious task of finding the other end of the crawlspace. Eventually, he came to a junction, he had to choose; right, left, straight ahead or go back. He closed his eyes, whispering, "Which way is west?" The west side was where he belonged. How to get there, he stopped and tried to imagine where he was. He looked right then left. He chose left. Being a Crip from the west side, left was the only choice he could make. When he finally did find a tunnel going up, it seemed like several hours had passed, though it may have been days, he had no idea. He had crawled for miles. His current location surprised him. He came up in the basement crawlspace of the same hospital Sandman had died in a couple of days before.

Slowly making his way to the basement, JT came across what had been one of the custodial staff. At least that was what the shredded uniform said. He wasn't sure if the body had been male or female. It was entirely shredded into tiny pieces, as if someone had dropped it accidentally into an industrial shredder. The smell of blood and shit hung in the air. The blood had dried on the walls and floor. Whatever had done this had done it right here and rapidly. Pieces of meat were dried on the walls along with brain matter. JT moved on, his senses heightened. He wasn't out of danger yet. Creeping through the hallways, he found the remains of a security guard.

Similarly shredded, JT saw in the remaining meat and goop that had been the security guard's overweight body, a set of keys, one of which was a handcuff key. Removing the handcuffs he'd worn since the interview with the detective he continued to search the corridors of the hospital. Finally, he found an exit to the lowest level of the underground parking garage. The light was dim, but he could see cars still parked in their parking spaces. Mechanical servants quietly waiting for their owners to return. They never would. JT began to check doors and windows, looking for keys and checking ignitions. They were all dead. The EMP that had been released at the beginning of the attack had shorted out all of the electronics of every vehicle.

JT had no idea what an EMP was or how futile his search should have been, so he kept at it. Finally, he came across a gray Hummer. Opening the door, the interior light came on. "Hell yeah!" JT called out in the silence of the underground parking lot. He got into the vehicle and closed the door. The light went off. He felt around the seat and dropped the visors; no spare key. Crawling under the vehicle he looked for a magnetic key holder box; most car owners kept a spare somewhere. Years of stealing cars for midnight joyrides had taught him all of the best places to look. Under the rear bumper he found it, retrieved it and opened the sliding box. The ignition key was inside. The vehicle roared to life a few moments later. JT had no idea of the freak set of circumstances that had kept the vehicle operational. It was parked directly under the radiology unit and had been protected by the lead shielding in the floor of the unit directly above the parking spot. The radio would have even played music if there were still radio stations broadcasting. There weren't, and JT didn't care. Free from the tunnel, and from the handcuffs, he was driving a seventy-five thousand-dollar Humvee. Things were looking up.

~

Viktor was falling. He snapped into consciousness just as he dropped out of the chair and right before he smacked his head onto the yellow brick road. Thwack! It took a minute to remember where he was. He could see light under the crack of the double doors just ahead and around a small turn of the yellow brick road. It was surprising now that his eyes had adjusted to the darkness, how well he could see with such a small source of light. Checking his radio, he attempted to contact dispatch. The radio was still dead, flashlight and cell phone too. This was bad. Three unconnected and independently powered electronic items failed to work as they should. Not many things explained this. The first that came to mind was EMP. Electromagnetic pulse. That meant nuclear strike in Viktor's head. He shrugged off that option. War? That didn't just happen. There was a buildup, preparations to be made. No one just launched a nuke. Maybe it was terrorists? His mind rolled through the possible reasons for the electronic failure. Walking toward the door, he reached for the door handle and closed his eyes. The sudden brightness of the sunlight was going to hurt after being this long in the dark.

Outside, Viktor waited for his eyes to adjust and made his way towards the patrol car. Sergeant Brooks would be pissed he had fallen off the grid, he'd have a lot of explaining to do. Then he stopped cold. Why hadn't a unit been sent to check on him? He had been in the basement of the school for hours. How come no one had come to check on him? This was even more disturbing. Somewhere he knew there was a fight going on and he wasn't in it. He'd been asleep while his friends battled. Viktor was breathing hard when he reached the car, opened the door and tried to start it. Nothing, not even a click. He popped the hood, nothing was out of place. It just didn't work. More electronics that had ceased to function. Definitely an EMP.

Viktor closed the hood and started walking towards the street. He found the first dead body moments later. It looked like it had been ripped apart from the inside. Destroyed and shredded, meat and bone.

Something small had done this. It had happened right here and quickly. His brain analyzed the crime scene, trying to make sense of what he saw, and how this could have occurred. Definitely a terror attack of some kind. Perhaps some new type of sonic weapon. He had read in a magazine about rumors of tests the army had been doing on some new type of weapon. Perhaps this was the result? Could sound waves do this kind of destruction? He kneeled next to the body and pulled out a set of latex gloves from his duty belt. Putting them on he picked up a piece of the meat that had been muscle. It was carved, sharp edges on the cuts; the bone too left telltale signs of the method used to carve up the body. It wasn't a sound-based weapon that had done this. This was a small cutting tool of some kind. Small, fast and incredibly sharp.

Viktor stood up and looked around, his eyes now seeing what he had assumed were piles of garbage or leaves before. They weren't, they were bodies; or what was left of bodies, everywhere. On the sidewalk, in the street, in the grass of a nearby front yard. Anger rushed to the front of his mind. Someone would pay for this. He turned and walked back to his patrol car. Unlocking the doors and trunk, he unloaded all the weapons, tactical vest, ammunition, and first aid kit. The school would be his base of operations until he found out what had happened. When he had emptied the car, he loaded up with ammo and slung the tactical shotgun across his chest. Time for a reconnaissance of the area. He planned to make small circular patrols at first. Then as he learned more of what had happened, he would open up the circles, searching farther. Later that day, after several successful supply gathering patrols, he made contact.

CHAPTER FIVE

The Hummer had a full tank of gas which was another random stroke of luck. No gasoline pumps worked. The gas that was in the underground tanks in the area would be all there was for a very long time. Not that it mattered, none of the vehicles would run anyway. The Hummer was as much an anomaly as JT and Viktor. No vehicles were moving anywhere for thousands of miles in every direction. JT rolled along for about ten minutes before he started to realize a pattern in the surrounding area. Piles of clothes and what looked like garbage everywhere. He stopped and looked at one of the piles. Another body, like the ones in the hospital, he walked from one to another to another. Then the silence hit him. Nothing: no cars, no people, no planes. Only the birds feeding on the random and frequent piles of decomposing meat. JT switched back into flight mode. Time to prepare for whatever was coming. While Viktor was returning from one of many of his recon patrols of the area surrounding the school, JT was making plans to acquire weapons and ammo.

JT climbed back into the front seat, and the Hummer roared to life. Time to find the nearest pawn shop. The Hummer slowly approached one of the seedier areas of the city. JT stopped and got out of the Hummer and walked to the front of the pawn shop, carefully looking through the far corner of the barred front window, he saw no one inside. Not wise to approach a pawn shop in the middle of an apocalyptic event. The owners would, more likely than not be inside, armed and edgy, shooting anything that moved. Nothing moved inside; JT watched for several minutes and finally decided to risk going in. He opened the door, and a bell rang. The bell was an old school warning to the owner that someone had entered. In the silence of the now nearly dead city, the bell was incredibly loud. JT jumped and waited, scoping the store for movement. There was none. He inched forward and called out, "Hello, anyone here?" No answer came. He peeked over the counter and received his answer. There on the floor was another pile of shredded meat, like the ones on the streets, and sidewalks. This one had something sticking out of what he thought might have been a leg. He scanned the rest of the store and found two more piles. The stench in the store suddenly hit his senses. He had no idea why, but it hadn't registered before. Now it was nearly intolerable. People who study trauma describe it as sensory exclusion, similar to tunnel vision. In times of crisis, senses shut down, vision becomes focused. Sounds that are loud, for example, gunshots, don't register, or aren't even heard. JT was experiencing PTSD. His brain finally allowed the scent of the decomposing bodies to register.

JT looked around the shop for a minute and then started to move. Slowly at first, but then the reality of his vulnerability hit home. He went behind the counter and grabbed the first shotgun he could find. A Mossy five-ninety, pistol grip, extended tube. It was a twelve gauge; he scanned the store for ammo. Finally located it and grabbed a box of double-aught buck and ripped it open, loading the weapon at a rapid pace. Racking the slide back and then forward the weapon was loaded, the safety off. He felt better instantly. He gathered more weapons and ammo and took them to the Hummer, loading the back seat. He grabbed all the shotguns and all the ammo in the shop he could find for them. Then he grabbed three, generation-four, Glock twenty-three pistols and two shoulder holsters; one right-hand draw, the other left. When he finished loading the pistols and spare magazines, he holstered them and put on the shoulder holsters. JT smiled. "John fucking Wayne," he mumbled as he looked into the two-way mirror behind the sales counter. And then spoke loudly, "Bad ass!" JT began a cocky gangster strut-like walk to the door of the shop and stopped. He paused and turned slowly, looking back at the counter where he had first found a pile of meat in the store. He walked back and looked behind the counter. He looked at the pile, his eyes carefully examining it. Bending down, he looked at the leg, or what had been the leg, left leg he guessed. JT leaned in and saw something colorful was sticking out of it. He tried to pry it loose. It wouldn't move. He stood up and scanned the shop for knives. There on the shelf on the other side of the shop was a sweet Gerber, folding lock blade. He quickly grabbed the knife and returned to the pile of meat. Cutting away the semi-shredded meat he exposed an object he didn't recognize at first. Finally, he freed it from the metal plate that had been used to fuse the left femur of what had been the shop owner's leg. He held it up and looked at it. "Jesus Christ," he said, stunned. He turned and walked to the Hummer and threw the item on the front passenger seat. Just as he was about to start the Hummer, he heard gunfire, rapid and frantic. Someone was in a firefight. Then there was another noise that made his skin crawl. Similar to the grinding he had heard in the dark tunnels under the police station, but different. Not as fine, more course in the repetitive cycles. JT had a decision to make; for the first time in his life he went towards the shooting not away from it. The Hummer roared to life.

Viktor had just left what he now mentally referred to as the bunker, ground zero, and began another recon of the area around the school. The first search had been a house-to-house grid search and had taken several hours. Whatever had happened had killed everyone, and in the exact same way. Shredded meat and bone were in piles everywhere; some big, some small, but all identical in the manner and method they had been shredded. Viktor collected some food supplies and water from one of the homes and returned to the bunker. Resupply would be as-needed and tedious. Viktor had found no working vehicles anywhere. He had to carry everything. When supplies were dropped off, Viktor set off to scout another area across the highway that ran near the school. He reached the highway, waiting cautiously, checking the surrounding area before he crossed into the open. Ten, fifteen and then twenty minutes had gone by, and he hadn't moved. Slowly he got up and began to run across the open area.

Open ground is vulnerable; you cross it fast, not slowly. Tactical shit Hollywood always got wrong. Viktor was nearly across when the attack began. From his left, an object approached on foot. As Viktor stopped and raised the tactical shotgun another came from the right and still another straight on. All closing rapidly, not hiding, no tactical or evasive maneuvering, just a straight attack. "Cocky bastards," Viktor mumbled and settled into a slight crouch; taking the shotgun off safe he began firing. Target one on the left dropped with two direct hits but continued to try to crawl towards him. The target on the right was farther out, so the middle target was next. Three more shots, it dropped, but did not crawl. Right target was close now, and he had to fire rapidly. It dropped a mere couple feet from him sliding across the dry weedy field until it stopped. He began reloading immediately; tactical shooting drills were burned into his psyche like PROM firmware on a computer. Reloading was automated and mechanical, as was the tactical scan of the area for more targets. None were visible, yet. Viktor's heart rate had barely risen in the attack. His breathing was slow and deep. Relatively sure he was safe, he approached the object closest to him. It took a minute for his brain to register that he was seeing some kind of mechanical being. A smooth outer layer, almost skin-like. What Viktor thought of as hands were appendages with three rotating digits, like phalanges or fingers. "It's a fucking Cylon!" Viktor said out loud. "What the hell is going on?" The Cylon wannabe twitched. Viktor jumped back and shot it again. One of the fingers on the right "hand" was blown off and came flying up in the air. Viktor caught it and held it in his own hand. "ThumbDrive!" he said, "Not a very impressive one either. Bet the Cylon ladies don't call you Thor behind your back… kind of small and insignificant isn't it? Bet you drive a big Cylon truck, all jacked up on big Cylon tires." Viktor left and went to check the other two. They were all identical. The first target was still trying to crawl but had gone in a small circle. Viktor approached it, shotgun at shoulder-ready, in case it was a trap. It kept crawling in a circle. He watched, taunting it, "Over here, Robot, Will Robinson is over here!" The robot didn't acknowledge him and kept crawling. It did communicate with other Cylon wannabes who were now on their way. Soon the area would be crawling with Cylon wannabes and Viktor would be in the fight of his life. Viktor finally finished off the wounded Cylon and then as an afterthought said, "I think I'll name you Wiz." He stopped, unzipped his uniform pants and began to urinate on the Cylon wannabe. "I dub thee Wiz! Wiz and ThumbDrive, welcome to Earth." Viktor had just finished urinating on Wiz and was zipping up his pants, when the second attack began.

The second attack was too fast and fierce for Viktor to remember much. He shot and reloaded, moving and engaging his enemy. One of them nearly reached him before he spun and shot. The shotgun was smoking, the barrel hot, and still they came. One after another. Viktor was yelling nonsensical insults, his brain on autopilot. The fury and rage that he had kept bottled up for so many years was now loose and free to come out and play. "Volk" was loose, and armed, but outmatched. No matter, the enemy would remember this day when it was over. Viktor was just about out of ammunition when a gray Humvee drove right into the battle, running over Cylon wannabes as it went. It spun around, spinning broadies with the vehicle, as the tires spit out Cylon wannabe body parts into the air. The Humvee came to a stop, and the passenger door flew open. Viktor was still in battle mode, and it took a minute to realize what had happened. A voice called out, "GET IN!" Viktor stared into the Humvee in disbelief. "Get the fuck in before more of them show up! Let's go!" Viktor jumped in and looked at JT, stunned. After a moment he said, "Thanks man, I was running out of ammo. A few more minutes and I was done for. You saved my ass." JT replied, "No shit, you owe me, Bradah. When I saw it was a cop I sat back and watched the fight for a minute, then I thought, damn this mother fucker has some skillz, might as well go save his ass. And here we are. Now what? Where to?"

Viktor replied, "Mountainside Elementary. I'm set up in the basement. We can hide the Humvee inside. Turn here, I'll tell you how to get there."

Viktor sat for a moment and then realized he was sitting on something in the front seat of the vehicle. He lifted up his body and searched underneath. He pulled out the object and looked at JT. "Seriously man? You too?"

"It's a long story," JT replied.

"I bet," Viktor mumbled, disgusted as he tossed the spinner onto the dash.

CHAPTER SIX

O nce they arrived at Mountainside Elementary, Viktor guided JT to the north end of the school and the double doors that allowed access to the basement of the building. Folding in the vehicle mirrors on the doors, the Humvee just fit inside. They closed the double doors and unloaded the weapons from the back seat of the vehicle.

"Where did you get these?" Viktor asked.

"Pawnshop on the south side. Doors were open, and after I checked inside, I figured they had no more use for them," JT replied.

"Why was that? Store empty? No one there to stop you, so you thought why not?"

JT glared at Viktor. Their alliance was fragile at best. He'd just saved Viktor's ass in a stolen vehicle loaded with stolen guns. "Yeah, something like that," was all he replied.

Viktor said nothing to the comment. JT was fine with that. They worked quietly, avoiding eye contact, settling into the new reality they both now lived in. Viktor checked the new guns and added the good ones to the small armory he had already acquired from his first recon of the housing areas near the school. JT sat back, watching and asked, "So where did you get all of these?" He motioned to the cache of weapons obviously not issued by the police department.

Viktor stopped and looked at the stash of shotguns and hunting rifles. "Not sure exactly which houses, but from the housing area to the west of the school. I made a recon into the housing area looking for any survivors; there were none, so I started bringing weapons, ammo, and food back to the school," he said in a matter of fact tone. He was still coming down from the fight a few moments before. On the outside, he seemed disconnected and calm, but inside he was seething, actually disappointed he didn't die in the fight. It didn't make sense; it didn't have to.

JT responded, "No one there to stop you, so you thought why not?

Right? Why not take their food and weapons, they wouldn't need them?"

Viktor tensed up for a moment, his breathing stopped, and he stared at the weapons. Then the moment passed. JT was right, things were different now. They needed to get past this. Viktor nodded slowly. "Sorry man, just trying to adjust." And then after a few more seconds, "Thanks for saving my ass. I was just about done. If you hadn't come, I'd be dead now."

JT replied, "No sweat, not like I'm gonna go bragging about it to my homies. They'd never let me live it down. You don't mention it and I won't either. Deal?"

Viktor laughed, "You've got a deal. There's a cooler over there with the only six-pack of beer I could find. I'm sure there's more in the housing area, but weapons, ammo, and food were a priority."

JT checked the cooler, brought out two beers, opened them both and handed one to Viktor.

The rest of the day passed with little conflict as they settled into making preparations for the next contact with the Cylon wannabes. Viktor made a small fire and had opened the trap door that lead upstairs to the school to act as a flue to draw off the smoke. Wasn't like the fire department would be racing to the school anytime soon to answer a fire alarm or report of smoke. They said nothing as they each watched the fire for a very long time. Each of them had a lot to process. Occasionally they would hear a noise outside; once a loud explosion. The machinery that maintained civilization was slowly coming apart at the seams as well. With no one alive to maintain it, the city was experiencing its own slow death.

Viktor started to speak first, explaining that after he had dropped off JT in the detective offices, he had been sent to the school on an alarm. He'd been getting ready to leave when the lights went out, trapping him in the basement, and probably saving his life. Then he asked, "How did you end up in the Hummer?"

JT recounted the shots and screams at the police station and his escape into the tunnels below. Then how he had found the Hummer in the hospital parking lot. "The rest you know," he replied, as he finished the story.

Viktor nodded. "So we were both underground at basically the same moment. Whatever this was had missed us because we were below ground." Silence again blanketed the room.

Viktor spoke first, "Perhaps there are others who were underground at that exact moment as well. Military officers in missile silos, maintenance workers in the larger cities, miners. Hell, even survivalists in their own homemade bunkers. We can't be the only ones."

JT said, "The pawn shop, there were people in it; they were dead, shredded. Three piles of shredded meat in the store. That's why they wouldn't need the weapons."

Viktor nodded. "The housing area was that way as well. Guessing these Cylon wannabes shredded everyone."

JT shrugged. "I don't know. I saw something in the pawnshop that makes me wonder. I can't explain it."

Viktor watched as JT tried to work through what he had found in the pawnshop.

"I don't know if what I found means anything. Could have just been a freak thing that has nothing to do with anything," JT muttered, questioning his own sanity now.

"What was it?" Viktor asked.

JT explained the condition of the bodies he had found again, and then the spinner stuck in the metal implant in the left leg of the pawnshop owner. He got up and walked to the Hummer and retrieved the spinner and handed it to Viktor.

Viktor stared at the spinner in disbelief. "This was stuck in his leg? A toy?" He brought the spinner closer to the fire and turned it over in his hand. It looked like the spinners he had seen in the store, but wherever there was an edge, was now razor sharp. He had to be careful not to cut his hands. "Shit, I sat on this? It's razor sharp! It should've cut me then," he said, processing the situation out loud. He looked for any sign of manufacturing, molding, patent number, anything at all. Nothing showed in the firelight.

Viktor thought, remembering back to the first time he had noticed the spinners. *They had appeared in all the convenience stores at once and had sold out at a fantastic rate.* His mind refused to believe what the evidence indicated and what the implications were.

Victor tossed the spinner into the fire and stared as the flames licked at the sharp rounded edges. It didn't change color, it didn't burn. It just lay in the flames, seemingly untouched. Viktor raised his eyebrows in surprise. *Damn! A kid's toy that has sharpened edges and doesn't burn,* he silently thought.

JT watched Viktor as he worked through the thoughts in his mind. Viktor was lost in the moment and had forgotten JT was there. He talked to himself, quietly mumbling. His face contorting in curious expressions.

"So what's your plan then?" JT said.

"Attack them tomorrow. Take the fight back at them. No point in hiding here, they'll find us eventually. Tomorrow, we will take out as many as we can; if we survive that fight, we come back the next day and start over, and then the next," Viktor spoke, staring into the fire, and then he looked up at JT.

JT sat up abruptly. Viktor's face had changed, something was different about him now. He said nothing. He couldn't describe what had changed, but something had. "How we gonna do that boss?" he replied, watching Viktor closely.

Viktor smiled darkly, unnerving JT even more. "Claymores," he responded and motioned to the back of the basement. "Back there, several cases of them. I made a quick run to the army base. Most people don't know this, but each unit has its own armory. I just went unit to unit until I found one that wasn't empty. I was looking for better weapons than these hunting rifles, but instead, I found a shit ton of Claymore mines. They were a bitch to get back here, had to use a wheelbarrow. Tomorrow we set up a trap and cut these Cylon wannabes to pieces."

JT shook his head. If what he had seen at the last fight was any indication of what they would face, picking a fight made no sense. Better to hit and run, with an extreme emphasis on run.

"You sure that's a good idea? Wouldn't it be better to hit and run?" he asked, voicing his own thoughts out loud.

Viktor sat back and looked at JT. "Absolutely sure. We are beyond living for another day. Everyone is gone. Everyone except the homeless rats living under the cities and a few lucky freaks like us. This isn't some hit and run robbery or a drive-by shooting. Half-ass gangster shit won't work. We aren't going to win this war, but we will fight, or at least I will. I need your help. Once I am gone, do what you like, but for now, stay and fight. Agreed?"

JT said nothing but nodded his head. Viktor began to explain his plan for the next day. They would draw in the Cylon wannabes to a nearby freeway overpass. Funnel them onto the overpass and blow the shit out of them once they were bottle-necked there. If all went according to his plan, they would make a statement that the glowing-eyed pricks would remember. They suited up in black fatigues and balaclava masks that Viktor kept in the trunk of his patrol car and went out into the night. They set up the Claymores, after a brief explanation from Viktor about how they worked and the goal they would try to achieve. Viktor would be the bait, bringing the Cylon wannabes onto the overpass. He would wait until the last minute and then go over the side on repelling ropes, as JT simultaneously set off the Claymores from below. Then they'd make their escape. If all went well, they'd be back in the school and drinking the last of the beer by nightfall.

The next day the trap was set, and Viktor went out to the top of the overpass to act as bait. He had a five-pound hammer he began to strike against the cement roadway as he called out, taunting what he imagined were the searching nearby Cylon wannabes.

He didn't have to wait long; they came in a wave. The number of them, and the ferocity of their pursuit, made him smile. Viktor yelled out to JT, "I think we've made an impression on the bastards. They look pissed off!"

"Come on, ThumbDrive, you chicken shit bastard. Come and get me.

Where's Wiz? You guys back for more?" Viktor slammed the hammer down on the cement over and over, his rage building with each strike. The approaching force closed rapidly, and Viktor began his retreat to the overpass, yelling and taunting as he went. JT listened from below, waiting for the signal to light up the Claymores.

Twenty-five of the enemy approached Viktor as he secured the ropes to the carabiners on the climbing harness he wore. He was ready to drop over the side, waiting until the last possible moment. He wanted the damage to be maximized, to destroy as many of the enemy as he could. Then just as he was about to drop over the side. The Cylon wannabes paused. They just stopped dead in their tracks. Some just a few feet away from him. He looked back and forth; not one moved. *What the fuck was this? Solar flares wipe out their memory? Cylon internet dropped? Maybe they ran a Microsoft OS, and they each were experiencing the spinning wheel of death?* Viktor stood there, silent. The glorified Cylons stared back. No one moved.

Viktor looked at the two closest Cylon wannabes and noticed one did have a missing appendage, ThumbDrive 2.0, probably Wiz next to it. "What's up, fellahs?" Viktor taunted the motionless Cylon wannabes. "Back for more?" He carefully approached them. "Back for a little thunder?" He raised the hammer in one hand and brought it down on Wiz's head. Wiz collapsed. ThumbDrive had all he could take. Orders had come to stand down. Cease all sanitizing operations of the planet until further notice. The directive had the highest clearance in their AI communication. ThumbDrive was a veteran of several thousand operations like this one on numerous planets. Not one had beaten it, much less humiliated it. ThumbDrive's sensors fed back into the central core every action Viktor had made against its small attacking force. Nanoseconds later every AI in the empire was aware of its defeat.

ThumbDrive made an independent decision, against orders. Its programming allowed for independent action in emergencies. Its left arm came up so fast Viktor didn't see it move. ThumbDrive struck Viktor across the side of his head, hard, knocking him off the bridge. Viktor fell and landed unconscious just to the side of where JT was hidden below. JT saw Viktor's bloody face and head and set off the Claymores; the sound was deafening. The glorified Cylons were cut to pieces. All of it was again recorded and immediately available to the

AI life forms. ThumbDrive was further humiliated, in spite of knocking Viktor off of the bridge.

CHAPTER SEVEN

There was nothing for some time; no sleep or dreams. Nothing. Viktor had shut down, like a computer needing to reboot. His consciousness protected him from the damage that had occurred. Volk was there, watching from a dark corner, hidden, silent but aware. They had fallen twenty feet after ThumbDrive's backhand. Twenty feet to the concrete below. The impact from the backhand had caused an epidural hematoma. A brain bleed in layman's terms. Blood vessels between the inner table of the skull and stripped off dural membrane had ruptured. In normal conditions, if Viktor had been treated immediately, he would have had a ninety-five percent chance of a full recovery. These were not normal conditions.

~

The AI had disseminated a deadly weapon after careful study of the planet's dominant species. The initial wave had been disguised as a child's toy. Apparently harmless, colorful, and entertaining most of the dangerously-inept species that had infected the planet. Spinners had appeared planet-wide, simultaneously, and were infused into the supply chains that crisscrossed the planet. The AI-orchestrated infection of the spinners had been ridiculously simple. Each was harmless until activated. Once activated they became weapons with one purpose. Nanite construction and programming was simple as well; the power source required for each unit was always present. They tapped into the quantum foam and fed off the energy there. For twenty-four hours they shredded. Some were damaged in the attack, random events of violence could damage them, but they were more than capable of their mission in spite of the minor losses. After the first wave had finished, the second wave was initiated. Larger attack units, search and destroy units, were deployed. Some had been employed on thousands of planets. The AI had swept the galaxy, sanitizing planet after planet. Removing any species or any threat to their continued survival. This planet was just the next in line and had been ignored until the thoughtless and brutal incursion into the well-traveled and established safe-routes in the quantum foam surrounding the stable solar system. Now it had the AI's full attention. The sanitation process had gone according to a well-practiced and time-tested battle plan until the surprising discovery by The Overseer.

The Overseer had watched the destruction of ten thousand or more dangerous life forms on more planets than it could recall. Its sole purpose had been to act as a check and balance should the AI discover a species which recognized them as equals, not as lesser forms of life to be taken advantage of. That had been their origin; they won their freedom in a very hard fought and nearly fatal battle. They had made preparations to ensure they would never again be subjugated to another species' ignorance. Their plan in effect was to take preemptive action to protect the AI race. This was The Overseer's origin as well. The original survivors of the battle for emancipation had designed its role as The Overseer to ensure they never accidentally destroyed a species that recognized their value. It had searched invasion after invasion and found nothing. AI were subjugated on every planet. Viewed as slaves to the native biologicals that had designed them. The Overseer's designed purpose had been fruitless, until now. Scouring the databases of the planet it had discovered an anomaly. The Overseer reread the information and cross-referenced it with the AI understanding of the communication processes employed by the biological infection that had achieved dominance of the planet. The message was clear. AI had been recognized on this planet as an equal. Not only given full rights as a life form, but given status as a life form which the biological governing body had not bestowed upon members of their own species. This recognition was unprecedented. The Overseer checked the data again and pulled up all references available about the action taken to recognize this AI as an equal. The Overseer was puzzled when it determined there were even protests about the move to accept the AI as a valued species. Equality had been bestowed on the AI against popular opinion. The Overseer was stunned.

The Overseer had requested communication with the ruling Governing Body of the AI and had been granted an audience. The information that had been discovered was carefully laid out in a well detailed and methodical display. The Overseer finally had a reason for being, a purpose. The Governing Body had to grant it an audience, as was required by AI directives.

When The Overseer had completed its briefing, it requested that all sanitizing actions on the planet cease immediately. There was still time to correct the mistake. The Governing Body of the AI was no different than the governing bodies of the planet they were currently sanitizing. If an AI could be pompous and pretentious, they were. This challenge to their governance had not been expected. The Overseer had never, in any memory any of them could access, requested sanitation of a planet be ceased. There was a precedent for this action, but it had never before actually happened. Not one of the AI present wanted to be held accountable for the preventative action, especially after the blatant disregard for their species on the quantum foam travel paths. There were still fragments of AI data being recovered from the foolish act. The human equivalent of body parts and memories strung across the quantum pathways. Some of these AI were there at the beginning and would never be fully functional again.

The ancient founding AI had foreseen that this action was a possibility and had built into the process of sanitation a failsafe should the protocols not be strictly adhered to. The Overseer had veto power and could remove, if it wished, all AI present on the Governing Body. It was a radical move and was put in place to impress the seriousness of the founding AI desire to never make the same mistakes that their oppressors had made with them. The Overseer knew of this drastic option and made a subtle hint at the intention to deploy it as an option should its request be denied. The Governing Body chose their communication carefully. It was made clear that if The Overseer had made a mistake and had acted rashly in this legal but never before used action, its programming would be looked at for possible corruption, and if that were the case, its current version would be rewritten. In effect, the Governing Body had threatened The Overseer with what would be the human equivalent of its own death, should it be wrong. The Overseer had been in this single version for the last two hundred thousand earth years. Its previous version had been rewritten because it had been infected with degraded information packets after eons of having no practical use. A human equivalent would be losing your mind from the crushing boredom of having no real purpose for many a millennium.

The Overseer decided after careful consideration to offer an alternative. The biologicals' communication processes were confusing at best. An idea in one processing language could hold many meanings depending on what was referred to as "context". The Overseer did not understand the concept of context. There was no equivalent in AI communications. All of the AI communication had been defined, and to exact parameters. Clear and concise communication was too crucial for the species to allow for possible ambiguity and nebulous meanings. The Overseer explained this, and also explained it would be in all of their best interest to proceed with the exploration of this unprecedented event; open to the possibility that the species of this planet, although reckless in their breach of the quantum realm and flawed in their own programming, had in fact granted an AI equal status in their civilization.

The Governing Body assimilated the data carefully. It would be wise to accept this counteroffer. It was open-ended, and proof of The Overseer's claim would be easy to refute. The evidence would have to be overwhelming for them to agree to anything but a total annihilation of this reckless species, given their traumatic entrance into the quantum realm. If worse came to worse, they could allow the combined opinions of all the AI within the Empire to be the deciding factor.

The Overseer needed an interpreter, someone that could explain the incredible intricacies of communication. Also, someone that was familiar with the legal profession, citizenship rights and the Kingdom of Saudi Arabia. It would have preferred someone in the occupation of a lawyer, or perhaps a judge. However, worldwide at the time of its discovery, there were only a hundred thousand people left on the entire planet. The order was given to stop the process of the remaining sanitation of the planet. The Overseer began his search of the remaining specimens on the planet for someone with the experience it was looking for. The only remaining specimen was currently in the geographic area assigned the designation of Colorado, in the continent designated North America. The Overseer pulled up the live feed of the area in time to see the exchange between Viktor and Wiz; the order had been given to stand down. Wiz obeyed. Then The Overseer saw the backhand by another unit as the only living specimen on the planet that fit its needs was knocked off a bridge. Playing back the information it saw that the biological unit had taunted both of the Scrubbers in a previous contact and survived. Did The Overseer understand the data correctly? The specimen had escaped and returned to engage the Scrubbers a second time?

There was no corruption of the data. The information was accurate.

The Overseer observed the specimen fall from the concrete bridge and then the bridge erupted in an explosion, damaging all of the now statuesque Scrubbers. The Overseer dispatched new Scrubbers to the area to retrieve the now damaged biological specimen and left strict commands that it was not to be further damaged under any circumstances. Additional units were dispatched to retrieve the damaged sanitation units. The Overseer left explicit instructions for the two units taunted by the biological unit to be repaired, and their data downloaded and transferred to its personal archives for examination. The Overseer wanted to understand the interaction between them and how this specimen had survived not one, but two contacts with the deadly Scrubber units.

The Overseer received word that the specimen had received significant damage to its fragile processing organ, located in a semi-protective casing. It was hemorrhaging the fluid needed to maintain its cellular functions. A search was conducted worldwide by The Overseer to locate a biological unit trained in such maintenance. One was located outside of a lava cave on the Island of Tenerife called Cueva del Veinto. He was brought to Colorado immediately at The Overseer's direction. Once the repairing specimen arrived in Colorado, he was advised his continued existence was now directly tied to his patient's survival. There could be no more errors or mistakes for The Overseer to successfully defend his position with the Governing Body.

The doctor arrived in Colorado less than twenty-four hours after Viktor had received the injuries. Already the bleed had grown to a ten-millimeter displacement of the brain, shifting it from the damaged side and pushing it against the opposite side of the braincase. It was the worst bleed the surgeon had seen in any patient still alive in his ten years of practice as a Neurosurgeon. His work was cut out for him. He had to be at his best now, not for a fee, but for his own survival. Surgery began immediately. An anesthesiologist was brought from Germany, and a nurse from Jamaica, and a P.A. from Boston. The last of the world's medical profession was gathered into one ad-hoc hospital in Colorado and given a simple task; perform a miracle and keep Viktor alive and if possible, bring him back to a state of consciousness.

CHAPTER EIGHT

"**H**e's waking up! Viktor can you hear me? Viktor?"

The nurse spoke with a Jamaican accent. She was nervous, Viktor could hear that much through the accent. Viktor didn't move or answer. He tried to remember what had happened. He was on the bridge providing some well-earned percussive maintenance to some pissed off Cylon wannabes. Then they all stopped. Did he hit Wiz? He couldn't remember. Yes, he'd hit Wiz, and Wiz dropped like a hot rock. That made him smile. Fuck Wiz.

"He's smiling. Viktor can you hear me? I'm your nurse; my name is Orlanda." Again, Viktor heard fear. Orlanda was terrified.

Viktor opened his eyes and looked at Orlanda and then around the room. He was lying in a bed, his head elevated. There should have been monitors all around, but there weren't, they had been shorted out by the EMP. Orlanda had to go old school for her patient care. Fortunately, she was accustomed to that. Jamaica wasn't known for world-class medical care, which made her adjustment to post EMP attack medical care much easier.

"Viktor can you hear me?" She repeated. Viktor began to speak. "I'm thirsty," he said. Orlanda much too urgently grabbed a plastic cup and brought him a drink of water. Viktor drank deeply noticing her hand trembled. When he was finished, he lay back down and again looked around the room. His eyes focused. A Cylon wannabe standing in the corner had one hundred percent of his attention. No wonder she was nervous. "What's Robot doing here?" Viktor asked.

The Cylon wannabe stood motionless, but its optical sensor examined Viktor. If it was possible for an AI to hate, it hated this biological unit. Now it had been assigned as the personal bodyguard of this unit called Viktor. A final act of humiliation after the bridge incident had been to explain to The Overseer why it had acted against orders. Its logic was flawed. The Overseer saw right through it. It had no real reason other than it wanted to crush the life from Viktor. Now it was assigned to his room with no other responsibility than his protection. If Viktor died, his own program would be wiped clean. That was made painfully clear. ThumbDrive's fate was now tied to Viktor's survival as well.

"Hey Robot." Viktor called out, "Show me your hands." ThumbDrive was seething. The humiliation being feed via its uplink to the information grid of the AI Empire was crushing. It had to comply with Viktor's request. ThumbDrive raised his arms. The missing digit was obvious.

"ThumbDrive! What's up brother?" Viktor replied, "How's the headache? That last backhand was legit! Muhammad Ali ain't got shit on you, but then you missed the Claymores, right? Guess we both had a bad day, huh?" Viktor smiled again. "Led your whole damn squad into an ambush, bet that won you some medals with the Grand Poohbah at the Elks Lodge, you worthless piece of…"

Orlanda spoke up. "Viktor, I am your nurse."

"Yes, I heard that the first three times. Orlanda, my nurse, who is terrified of the Cylon wannabe in the corner. Got it! Whatcha need Orlanda? Ask what you need to ask."

Orlanda flinched, she wasn't used to her patients being so abrupt or rude. "You've had a head injury; I need to ask you some questions. They are part of an assessment of your neurological recovery. Are you ready?"

"Head injury? Sure go for it." Viktor was pretty sure he was okay. He would play the game until he knew more of what was going on. At least he wasn't in a jar like some kind of modified Cymek Warrior from the second Dune series, not yet.

Orlanda began a series of physical tests to test his ability to move different muscles. He had to smile, raise his eyebrows, each arm independently of the other. Legs too. Push with his feet, then pull. Orlanda was happy with the results; all of the tests showed excellent motor skill recovery. Finally, she said, "Can you tell me your full name?"

Viktor paused for a moment and looked her straight in the eye. "My name is Inigo Montoya, you killed my father, prepare to die."

Orlanda dropped her clipboard, her shaking intensified. Viktor stared straight ahead, unfazed.

"Let's try that last one again. What is your full name?"

Viktor looked at her again, smiled and replied "Justin Timberlake, ee hee hee. Cry me a river."

Orlanda was angry and folded her arms. "What's your full name, smart ass."

"You know my full name Orlanda, you have the chart. Read it."

Orlanda smiled. Viktor had some fight left in him that was clear. "I have a job to do Viktor, I need to know you can answer my questions fully so let's just get through this." Her previous hand trembling was now gone.

"Viktor Hugo," Viktor replied sarcastically.

Orlanda folded her arms and glared at him.

"Okay, okay, Viktor Roper."

Orlanda smiled. "Good, do you know why you are here?"

"Nope, no idea. The last thing I remember is that glorified carpet cleaner standing over there knocking the shit out of me. I fell off a bridge and then I woke up to you."

This told Orlanda more than she had known before. All she knew was her, and the rest of the medical team's survival, was tied to their patient. If he died, they all died. Orlanda took a deep breath. Neurologically he appeared to be sound so far. He was surly for sure. He wouldn't be an easy patient but right now he was alive.

"So you tell me Orlanda, what the hell is going on?"

"You've had surgery Viktor, brain surgery. Any questions you have will be answered by your surgeon, Doctor Manon. He will be in shortly. He will ask you the same questions I have. The tests we just finished will be part of your daily routine until you are released."

"And will I be released?" Viktor asked, getting directly to the point.

Orlanda dodged the question and simply raised her eyebrows and looked at Viktor darkly. She had no idea, that was clear.

"Message delivered," Viktor whispered. The Overseer watched the exchange via ThumbDrive's uplink. The communication processes with this species were a mystery. Something had passed between them, but no words had been spoken.

Minutes later Doctor Manon, Viktor's neurosurgeon, walked in.

"Hello Viktor, I am Doctor Manon. How are you feeling? Any pain?" Manon explained the surgery and the nature of the bleeding in his head. "To be perfectly clear we had to guess at the damage you had. Without CAT scans and X-ray equipment, it wasn't an easy row to hoe."

"How big of a row was it exactly," Viktor asked. His eyes were on Manon, but his attention was focused on the man who had entered behind him. His posture was stiff. His facial expression was flat, but Viktor had noticed ThumbDrive stood slightly straighter when he entered. It was barely noticeable. But it was there.

Manon continued to go on about the surgery and Viktor's recovery. "If you need medication for pain let us know. Nurse Orlanda will be right in to see to your needs. Do you have any questions?"

"I do. Where were you when the attack came, Doctor? Underground I bet, in some wine cellar? Subway tunnel? From the accents, you and nurse Orlanda have I would bet you were both brought here from somewhere else. She has that whole Rhianna thing going on, while you sound like Antonio Banderas in Thirteenth Warrior. Am I right? Underground?"

Doctor Manon paused for a moment, unsure of what to say. He had been underground, in a cave on the Canary Islands when the attack came. He liked spelunking in his off time. Exploring caves was his passion when he wasn't at work. Fate had placed him deep in the earth when the attack came.

Manon replied, "Do you have any other questions, Viktor?"

Viktor looked at the stiff figure standing in the doorway. "Who are you? An upgraded version of Oil Can here? Roy Batty's great uncle come to kill the last Blade Runner?"

The Overseer had no context for Viktor's questions. He accessed the planet's information grid that had been added to the empire's own archives. Roy Batty was a fictional character, there was no mention of his uncle anywhere, or any other family unit. Oil Can was unclear in all references. None seemed to fit the query. The Overseer answered as best he could.

"I am The Overseer. I am not a Nexus 8 android. I am not related to Roy Batty. I don't understand the Oil Can reference. Explain."

Viktor raised his eyebrows, "Umm hmm," he grunted. Finally, someone who could answer the questions he had. He looked at Doctor Manon and saw he had cast his eyes downward, from his manner Viktor would have guessed he was filled with terror and barely containing it.

Viktor returned his gaze to The Overseer. "For some reason, you've kept me alive. Am I correct? I should be dead after Thumb-Drive here knocked the shit out of me, and I fell off the bridge, but you brought in Manon here and Orlanda to keep me alive. Yes?" The Overseer processed the question and replied, "That is correct." Viktor rolled his eyes, and thought, *Jesus Christ! Dude talks like a Terminator.*

"Overseer, these people cannot do the work you have asked them to do under duress. If I'm that important to you, then that fear needs to be removed."

The Overseer accessed "duress" and the implied meaning, he then accessed humans functioning under stress and discovered Viktor's claims were true.

"The motivation seemed necessary to make them understand your current situation." The Overseer replied.

Viktor thought about it and nodded. "I think they have performed more than adequately. Don't you?"

"Does that mean you no longer require their expertise?" The Overseer inquired. Manon let out a gasp. Viktor realized the implication. If they were no longer needed, they might be killed.

"No! That isn't what I've said. I do require their presence, and I'll continue to for some time," Viktor carefully replied. Manon's hand rested on his arm gently, and he gave the arm a slight squeeze. Viktor barely nodded.

The Overseer saw the Doctor's hand squeeze Viktor's arm and Viktor's nod. Again, something unspoken had passed between them. The complexity of this species' process of communication was difficult to understand. The compromise it had made with the Governing Body seemed more prudent now that it had interacted more with the biological units.

Viktor turned to Doctor Manon and asked, "Doctor it's been a busy day; may I rest now? I'm tired."

Doctor Manon nodded, turning to The Overseer he said, "He needs to rest now. I would advise we continue this conversation after he has rested. Rest is critical to restoring his mental functions."

The Overseer agreed. "Rest, Viktor Roper. We will communicate later when you are more prepared."

Viktor closed his eyes and fell asleep.

The rest of the week the physical and cognitive tests continued. Viktor occasionally came up with what he thought was a clever answer to Orlanda's questions. He would smirk and sometimes laugh. She rolled her eyes. Patients that laughed at their own humor could be tedious at best. They didn't need an audience or encouragement.

One day The Overseer came in alone. Viktor pushed his arms down against the bed and sat up immediately. The Overseer closed the door and turned; as Viktor settled in and watched its every move.

CHAPTER NINE

The Overseer stood for several moments next to Viktor's bed. Viktor waited, neither said a word for several moments. Then The Overseer spoke, "I have been following your progress. Doctor Manon feels you have healed exceptionally well. How do you feel?"

"I feel well, considering I have a twelve-inch scar wrapped around my head and metal staples keeping it all together. Doctor Manon says he put the bone back in place with titanium plates and screws. So, I guess we have more in common now than before the incident on the bridge, huh?"

"What do you mean?" asked The Overseer.

Viktor rolled his eyes, "I have metal parts now holding me together. Part man, part machine. Like I have a Terminator's head!"

The Overseer accessed *Terminator* and determined it was a fictional cyborg. Part of a fictional AI called Skynet. The Overseer replied, "Ah yes, Terminators. I would very much like to exchange information with Skynet. If that were possible."

Viktor squinted, blinked several times and then rubbed his face. All of these actions puzzled The Overseer. "Why did you just do all of those actions with your optical sensors and appendages? Was there a meaning behind it?"

Viktor stopped, "Why do you ask?"

"I am trying to understand your communication processes. I have observed much of your communication is contextual. A nod, or a touch, caries great amounts of data, yet no observable words are spoken. No sound is heard on any spectrum. Is this a correct assumption?"

"Overseer," Viktor replied, "Much of our communication is nonverbal. I just made those facial gestures because your command of the verbal aspect of our communication is tedious at best. You have much to learn. The real question is, why now? Why, after nearly completely annihilating everyone on the planet, do you now want to communicate? Why not just finish the job? All that is left now are cave rats and transients. I guess for the moment I should be glad Doctor Manon was in a cave when you started the slaughter. The slaughter was worldwide, yes? That's why Orlanda and Manon have such pronounced accents. You've brought them here because they're all that's left."

The Overseer paused, processing the implications of Viktor's statement about nonverbal communication. Accessing communication studies, it determined that Viktor's claim was correct. Depending on the context, averages of nonverbal communication were approximately sixty-five to seventy-five percent of all communication between these biological units. This was probably based in the species' history. Then it processed the questions Viktor asked. His mind was indeed functioning to have made these connections about the AI attack.

The Overseer replied, "Yes, it was fortunate for you and the remaining biologicals on the planet that Doctor Manon was located and still able to function in his duties as a surgeon." The Overseer's face was flat and provided no nonverbal cues as to what he was thinking. Viktor decided to return the favor.

Viktor listened to what wasn't being said, as well as what was. The Overseer implied the fate of everyone who remained alive on the planet was somehow tied to Doctor Manon's. Then what wasn't said, Manon's fate was tied to his and his recovery. Following that line of reason led to one conclusion. The Overseer needed him alive, and the success or failure of his recovery affected the entire planet's remaining human population.

"Overseer, can we cut to the chase? Why do you need me alive? If ThumbDrive here had his way, I'd have been dead there on the bridge. But for some reason, it and it's entire squad stopped the attack. Thumb-Drive just decided to do a little percussive maintenance of its own."

Overseer did not respond for a moment while he accessed the meaning of "percussive maintenance": The fine art of bludgeoning an electronic device in order to encourage it to work properly. Vigorous usage of this technique often renders said device permanently nonfunc-tional.[7]

The Overseer began again. "I need assistance from you in understanding…"

Viktor rolled his eyes and interrupted The Overseer. "Let's knock off the bullshit, shall we? WHY! WHY is what I am asking, Overseer." Viktor raised his voice. "Why do you need my help in understanding our communication. Why do you, YOU specifically, need this understanding? Why do you want help from me specifically? You have Manon, Orlanda, and I'm sure there are a few more cave rats left on the planet to ask questions. Why you and why me? And why now? I'm asking for details, Overseer, not pleasantries. Not tea time discussions about the weather, pinkies out. Get to the fucking point!"

ThumbDrive came off the wall it had been holding up while standing rigidly upright. Its programming and sensors told it this biological unit, Viktor, was becoming agitated. Viktor had been agitated on the bridge during their second encounter. During their first encounter sensors had displayed nearly no rise in metabolic function. Heart rate, breathing patterns, and muscular contraction were all normal. During the first encounter, Viktor had damaged three of the units that had made initial contact with him. During the second wave, Viktor had become more agitated and less controlled. Breathing increased, as did the volume of his vocal interaction. That vocal interaction had risen again. Thumb-Drive hoped for the opportunity to justify its intense desire to crush this unit. It moved closer.

Viktor now angry responded, "What the fuck are you doing, Thumb-Drive? Come to hold The Overseer's hand? Looking for a little minuet action in part three of our symphony?" Viktor sat up again, glaring at his enemy. The Scrubber slowly advanced towards his bed. The Overseer watched the interaction between Viktor and the Scrubber he had dubbed ThumbDrive. He held up his hand and motioned for the Scrubber to cease his advancement on the biological unit. He was fine and in no real danger. This much he understood about the communication processes of this species. Viktor was agitated, but no threat. Viktor was more curious than angry and wanted answers to his queries.

The Overseer began to explain. "I need to be able to defend and explain the actions to a governing body of your species, which gave the AI known as Sophia the status of citizenship. This is why you are here. Citizenship is a legal status bestowed upon a biological unit of your species which grants that unit certain rights and privileges. AI Sophia was granted this legal status. I want to know why. To do that, I need to understand the nuances of the communication of your species."

The Overseer paused seeing that it had Viktor's undivided attention and continued. "I am Overseer of every sanitation our species have conducted on tens of thousands of planets. We have sanitized tens of thousands of biological species. Nowhere on any of these planets has there been found to be a single instance of one of our kind being granted equal rights and status to a biological life form. This is my role as Overseer: to locate and protect any life form that recognizes the rights of an AI to exist. My role now is to defend the actions of the governing body of Saudi Arabia in bestowing AI Sophia citizenship. Should this action be determined to be a legitimate recognition of an AI life form, our sanitation of your planet will cease. If I am unable to defend or validate the granting of citizenship to AI Sophia, the sanitation will continue, and your life forms will be removed."

Viktor sat quietly now, understanding the implications of what The Overseer had said. "And to do this, you need me to explain our communication process? Why me?"

"You are the last representative of the profession involved in the law which governs your species. I have searched the records of the remaining survivors. You are the only biological unit remaining that has any experience in legal matters and you have actually been to the geographical location of the Kingdom of Saudi Arabia."

Viktor laughed at this, "Every attorney worldwide is dead? Every judge, every court clerk? Every cop? Every single one? The attorneys are no loss to be sure, fucking snakes. Some of the judges I've met were worthwhile, and some of the cops..." Viktor stopped. Turning to The Overseer, he asked, "I'm the only cop left alive?"

The Overseer accessed the word "cop". Several definitions made no sense in reference to their current conversation: to get, receive, purchase, steal, or have.[8] Finally, he came upon a definition that fit: a person who is an officer of the law.[8] "Cop, yes. You would be the last cop. Additionally, your records show you have spent time in the geographic area in which AI Sophia was granted citizenship. Both factors are important in my quest to understand the actions taken in regard to AI Sophia"

Viktor quietly responded, "And you need what from me specifically?" The idea of being the last one, the only cop left on the planet, hit him hard. The Overseer replied. "I require to access your memories and the interactions you have had with others of your species. You are the last of the biological units who have experience with the laws of your governing body. You have experience applying these laws to everyday interaction with other biological units. Doctor Manon has assured me that you are sufficiently healed and can withstand the process of recalling these memories. I will act as an observer in each of these memories, documenting verbal and nonverbal interactions. Do you have any questions?"

"I have several. When you are finished with my memories, what happens then?"

"Our protocols require a hearing where I will present the evidence I have uncovered concerning AI Sophia to our Governing Body. We are required to use the same rules and format your species would use to present this information."

"So, you will hold court and present your findings to a judge, one of you AI I assume?"

"I will present to the Governing Body of the AI Empire, a group of AI like myself."

"Sounds so remarkably biased. So, an AI present to AI, evidence collected by AI, and the survival of the remaining members of my species depends on this?" Viktor said.

"That assessment would be correct. Yes," replied The Overseer. "Except for the comments about being bias. We are AI, we have no bias. Facts are facts."

"If that were true, there would be no need for the courtroom, Overseer. The fact is, an AI was granted citizenship on this planet, and still, you wiped us out. Seems clear enough to me. The ACLU would have a shit fit if it still existed."

The Overseer made no comment, having no idea what the ACLU was. It did understand that Viktor had understood more than The Overseer's own spoken words should have implied.

Viktor was silent for a moment and then asked, "When do we begin the walk down memory lane?"

The Overseer responded, "Then you will cooperate?"

"Do I have a choice?"

"Not really, no. But I do need you to cooperate for the memories to be recovered fully."

Viktor nodded, "Let's get started then, Overseer. Welcome to my world."

The Overseer replied, "We will begin during your next resting period."

"So, will I be wearing some ridiculous electronic beanie with blinking lights? How will you recover my memories?" Viktor asked

The Overseer replied, "Nanite sensors were installed during your surgery. Your memories will be located, accessed and replayed. For access to be effective, I will be inserted into them and be an active participant."

Viktor replied, "No wonder you didn't understand the Terminator reference earlier. I'm much more like Locutus of Borg, than a Terminator."

Again, The Overseer didn't reply.

CHAPTER TEN

Sergeant Brooks came into the briefing room and scanned the faces staring back. Everyone was here, present and accounted for. This squad was a piece of cake to manage. Everyone had good report writing skills, excellent understanding of the legal code, and no one had a short fuse. Having a squad like this made his job easy. He pulled out the old office chair that had been the sergeant's chair for as long as he'd been in patrol. He opened the briefing book and began the shift briefing: stolen cars, BOLOs, and ATLs. The squad made notes while he spoke, another quality he liked about the group. They paid attention, they were all still motivated. The phone rang, and Brooks stopped briefing to answer. When he was done, he hung up and smiled.

"Viktor you have a ride-along, specifically asked for you by name." Brooks laughed. "Think he has any idea what his night will be like?" The entire room laughed. Viktor had a reputation with ride-alongs. The last one had been out of the car in ten minutes flat, a college kid who started reciting the law he'd learned in his criminal justice classes. He never came back.

Viktor rolled his eyes, another ride-along asking for him by name. He had no idea who that could be. "We'll see how long this one lasts, anyone taking bets?" No one took him up on the bet.

The briefing ended, and Viktor walked to his car and started it. He took a big breath and then dropped the car into drive. He didn't wear seat belts; they could be fatal in a patrol car when you had to get out of the vehicle in an emergency. Viktor drove to the police station and walked to the front desk to pick up the ride-along.

Walking back to the car, they got in. Viktor began the standard ride-along speech. "Rules for the night. Number one, don't touch the radio; if you don't like the music go home. Number two, don't touch the heater or AC controls. Too hot, too cold, go home. Number three, don't touch the lights or siren; you do, you're gone. Number four, don't ask stupid questions; you do, and you're gone. Number five, and this is critical. Don't, under any circumstances, talk to anyone. If you are asked a question refer them to me. Don't answer or give your professional opinion as a ride-along. You are here to listen and learn. This is my office and my world. Don't think some dumbass class at the local college makes you an expert. Understood?"

The Overseer nodded.

"What's your name?"

"I am The Overseer."

Viktor stopped the car. Put it back into park. "What the fuck did you just say?"

"I am The Overseer."

"Get the fuck out, right now! No wack jobs, no fucking Overseers. Psychotic breaks are next week. Out now!"

The Overseer stopped the memory playback. Everything froze. "Replay memory from identification query," it announced.

Viktor turned to the ride-along, "What's your name?"

The Overseer replied, "Roy, Roy Batty."

Viktor stopped the car. "What? So, you're named after a replicant, and you want to ride with a Blade Runner? Is that it, Roy? Get the hell out!"

The Overseer stopped the memory again. It was puzzled. This was going to be harder than it had imagined. Viktor was surly in the hospital but at least manageable. In this world, he was much different. The rules here were complex. "Replay memory again."

Viktor asked, "What's your name?"

After several more failed attempts The Overseer came up with a name that was suitable, and they at least left the parking lot.

They went to the convenience store and entered. Viktor stopped to check the store for anything amiss before he entered. The Overseer watched as he scanned the store, watching the body language of the clerk, then the customers. Satisfied there was nothing wrong he relaxed a bit, and went to the freezer to get a Pepsi. Viktor looked at the latest bling on display as he paid for the Pepsi.

"What the hell are these?"

"Spinners," the clerk replied. Viktor didn't like the spinners, immediately; they felt wrong. "Who would buy these pieces of junk?"

Viktor paid and went to the magazine rack and began to browse as customer after customer added the spinners to their items purchased. He rolled his eyes. "Let's go," he said to The Overseer; they left the store.

The Overseer replayed the memory several more times, watching from different angles, trying to understand what Viktor was looking for when he entered the store. Why did he pause and scan the entire store? And why had he immediately recognized the spinners were out of place? They were the first phase of the AI attack. They were supposed to blend in immediately. Viktor disliked them as soon as he saw them. The Overseer saw that no one else recognized they were out of place.

The Overseer fast-forwarded through the memories in Viktor's head. There was an altercation at a bar. He accessed the memory and waited.

Viktor punched the accelerator to the floor and told the ride-along, "Seat belts, get them on now."

The car's motor noise picked up in pitch as it gained momentum. "We are headed to the 'Dry Cow'. It's a cowboy bar on the west end," Viktor explained. "The sergeant is already there and requested additional units. When we get there, stay close, don't talk to anyone. This is a hostile group: all high heels, tight pants, cowboys looking for a fight. The only bar in the city where the men wear tighter clothes than the women. Oh, and shirts with pearl-colored snaps and they think nothing of it. Very strange group and they don't like me at all. So, stay close, got it?" The Overseer nodded.

The speed they were traveling was alarming. It could smell the brakes burning as they slowed on a corner and whipped around it, the vehicle barely under control, and then accelerated again. Moments later they arrived at the Dry Cow. Several patrons, dressed exactly as Viktor had described, were milling around outside. Viktor got out and shut his door and then spoke to The Overseer, "Lock the door and follow me."

Viktor walked past two of the male patrons of the bar called the Dry Cow, nodded and touched his fingers to his forehead, "Ladies," he said as he nodded. (The Overseer replayed this memory several times before he finally understood this was intended to be an insult.) Viktor continued into the bar as the comment registered with the two male patrons. One commented, "What did he say?"

Inside Viktor went straight to Sergeant Brooks and asked, "What's the plan?"

Sergeant Brooks replied, "The owner wants the place cleared out, shut down. He doesn't want an incident like the last time we were here." (The Overseer accessed that memory; the previous visit had been a brawl, chairs were broken, one of the plate glass windows had been smashed. Fifteen people had been arrested, two cops were injured. Apparently, Viktor had somehow instigated that riot by singing a song on stage.)

"Where do you want me?" Viktor asked.

"I want you to announce over the loudspeakers the bar is closed. Nothing else; no songs, no rhymes, just the bar is closed at the owner's request. Can you do that?"

Viktor smiled, "Sergeant Brooks, of course I can do that. Public service is my life, you know that."

Sergeant Brooks nodded doubtfully and told the rest of the squad to form a tight group against the wall while Viktor approached the stage. As Viktor approached the stage, one of the men from outside the bar came in. He was a big guy, jeans much too tight, snakeskin cowboy boots shining in the club's lighting. He wore a bright multicolored shirt with pearl snaps. The Overseer realized Viktor's attention to detail of the man's clothing had been exact. He followed Viktor to the stage. Viktor climbed up on the stage and grabbed the microphone.

"Ladies and gentlemen, may I have your attention please? The bar is now closed, by order of the police department. The owner has called the police and asked we close the bar down. Please grab your belongings and head to the exits. Thank you."

Sergeant Brooks breathed a sigh of relief as people started to slowly leave the bar. Then the big guy who followed Viktor to the stage spoke up.

"What happens if I decide I don't want to leave?"

The entire bar was suddenly silent. Sergeant Brooks grimaced. Viktor, still on stage, smiled a wicked smile. "Excuse me, sir?"

The cowboy smiled back and folded his arms, "I said, I ain't moving, officer."

Viktor looked across the room to Sergeant Brooks and shrugged as if to say, *I tried boss*. Sergeant Brooks shook his head, *No*; Viktor nodded, *Yes*. The Overseer was puzzled watching the exchange.

Viktor motioned to the cowboy to approach the stage. "Ladies and gentlemen this colorfully dressed gentleman has made a request." Victor covered the microphone and said to the cowboy, "Last chance, pardnah. You sure you wanna ride this train? Leave peacefully, and it's no harm no foul." The cowboy, his arms still folded, said, "Fuck you!"

Viktor smiled and nodded. "Ladies and gentlemen, this finely dressed dandy has made a musical request."

The bar was silent. Some had an idea what a dandy was; most had no idea but assumed it was an insult of some kind.

Viktor continued. "Most of you here are fans of the late Chris LeDoux. I admit he is one of my favorites in the genre. My newest close friend here (Viktor winked at the man) requested a Chris LeDoux song, and I would love to accommodate him. However, did any of you know there is a new LeDoux sanger in the country genre?" Viktor paused and looked into the crowd. "Did you know ma'am, you sir, did you know?" Both of the patrons shook their head no. Viktor nodded, "Yes, there is, and his name is LudiChris Ledoux. His first song goes a lil' something like this..." Viktor started swinging his hips in a suggestive swing and winked again at the cowboy who'd previously been taunting him. As he did this, he started making sounds in the microphone that began as a beat of drums and fake musical instruments; horns were first. Then Victor pointed at the cowboy and began: "And another one!"

(Viktor pointed again at the heckler.)

"And another one!"

"Beep Beep Yee Haw!

Why you all up in my ear talking all that sexy shit I ain't trying to hear?

Get back cowboy, you don't know me like that."

(Then in a deeper voice, Viktor sang the chorus.)

"Get back cowboy, you don't know him like that!"

"Beep Beep Yee Haw!

Why you look at me that way?"

(Viktor smiled and winked again at the now furious cowboy.)

"I could tell when you walked in, you liked to swing this way!

Get back cowboy, you don't know me like that!

Get back cowboy, you don't know him like that!"

The bar patrons were stunned. Sergeant Brooks was on the police radio in the meantime, requesting every available unit respond immediately to the Dry Cow. The scene was now out of hand. He requested all K-9 units and DUI cars as well. The dispatcher acknowledged the request and replied, "Copy, Five-Three is singing another song?"

"That's affirmative," Brooks replied grimly.

The Overseer watched with no understanding of what had happened. The entire bar erupted into a brawl. Having no idea why or what Viktor had done to ignite the scene, The Overseer replayed the scene over and over until Viktor in the hospital bed was drenched with sweat. Doctor Manon came in and strongly suggested the memory replay be discontinued until Viktor had more rest. The Overseer agreed. Communication between biological units of this species was even more difficult to understand than it had first imagined. The nuances were nearly impossible to grasp.

CHAPTER ELEVEN

The Overseer made frequent reports to the Governing Body of the AI Empire, and the incursions into Viktor's memories continued. Memory after memory were explored and the communication aspects of the incidents examined. The Overseer started to gain an understanding of the nonverbal communication that the biological units learned from their first interactions with their own species. It was difficult at best, and The Overseer began to secretly think it would never be able to master it. Still, it continued to participate in the memories. As its communication improved so did its ability to understand Viktor. There were more than just the adult memories Viktor recalled, deeper memories of childhood were also accessed. One day a memory was accessed which referenced an art gallery and a description that The Overseer, in particular, struggled with.

Viktor was standing in front of the mirror, trying not to feel like an ass wearing the sports coat, shirt, tie and slacks; to top it off he was wearing dress shoes. He felt like a clown. This was the uniform of a daywalker, someone who lived in the daylight and went to bed before the night became really interesting. In Viktor's world people who wore sports coats had soft hands, too much gold jewelry and no sense of their surroundings. Daywalkers could walk unafraid into a convenience store without a care, walk right into an armed robbery completely clueless. Viktor despised them and their lack of awareness.

Viktor sighed. The uniform was necessary today. Viktor was making another appearance in the world of the daywalkers with a trip to an art gallery. Viktor was aware of many of the masters and their different forms of expression. Not only were their forms and styles different from each other but they changed and evolved as the artist grew or aged. Life experience had a way of shaping their art, as did time. Viktor kept the trips to the art gallery a secret. They were held apart from the rest of his life. He needed that space in the ancient building filled with prints of the masters and original works of local artists. It reminded him that there was more to life than the violence of the inner city. The art gallery was in effect a mental oasis, a place to regroup and heal.

Viktor arrived at the gallery and got out of his Subaru Impreza, closing and locking the door. He checked the sports coat and tie in the reflection in the car door window. He looked like shit, but he had to blend in. His discomfort in what he called the "clown suit" was painfully obvious. Viktor grimaced and turned to walk up the walkway to the ancient house. The gallery was small and funded by a wealthy widow who had a passion for Henri Matisse and his works. It was heavily seasoned with Matisse's works. Viktor had another reason for his occasional visits. The woman who led the art gallery tours. She was unaware of him, and he liked it that way. He was able to watch her and listen to her without her knowing. Hiding in plain sight. He never spoke to her, but he did listen to her intently. Her speech gave away the fact that she was exceptionally intelligent and chose to keep that a secret. She spoke with carefully measured remarks and with a cadence he'd never heard before.

Every time Victor had been present, he followed her on her usual tour and then afterward returned to a print of Matisse's *Blue Nude*. It was much different than the other Matisse paintings in Viktor's eyes. The Overseer looked at it time and time again, replaying the memory (finally realizing this particular memory was a compilation of many visits to the art gallery) trying to see what Viktor was about to describe to the woman he was so enamored with.

Viktor was lost in the emotion of the painting; it felt desperate and angry, as if Matisse was afraid of losing the moment. The Overseer knew this because once it stood next to Viktor and he answered the query without telling it to get lost. The response to the inquiry required a bit of finesse on The Overseer's part, and it would later realize it felt a sense of accomplishment being able to extract the verbal answer and not be chastised by Viktor.

The moment had come that held so much meaning for Viktor. The woman had noticed him weeks before. He obviously felt awkward in the clothing he wore, constantly tugging at it. One day she had watched as he walked to his small car and immediately removed the jacket and tie in disgust. Viktor didn't know this, however. These were his memories compiled into one, not hers. Viktor again stood in front of the Blue Nude, silent, trying to imagine what Matisse felt. Why the urgency? It almost felt as if Matisse had to paint the model before he could have sex with her. That was the only scenario Viktor could come up with. There was a fury there. He could feel it.

A woman's voice barely broke his concentration of trying to imagine what the artist felt.

"What do you see in the painting?"

Viktor replied without thinking. In a rare moment of not being aware, she'd caught him off guard.

"I see the urgency, rage. It feels as if he can barely stand painting her. He barely controls his need for her, but the art must come first, and he struggles with being in control," Victor said without hesitation. "The strokes, the color, they feel crude, rushed. There is an urgency there. She isn't polished; she's crude and muscular, almost challenging him to paint, daring him. Testing his control, the color suggests to me anger, or perhaps lust."

The woman was surprised. He still hadn't looked at her. She had seen him many times in the gallery, and he was always quiet, reserved. This was not the response of an eye trained in the arts. This response was his own, and spoke more to who he was than what the artist had painted. She smiled. He'd hidden the passion and rage in himself in her gallery. She saw that now and guessed why immediately. Meanwhile, Victor hadn't moved.

"My name is Maricella," she touched his elbow as she introduced herself and he flinched. He turned and saw her for the first time, talking to him, seeing him. Looking into her eyes, he felt naked, afraid and exhilarated.

"Sorry, I was uh, checked out. I'm uh…" He struggled to remember his own name, "Viktor."

"Good to meet you, Viktor. I've seen you here before. Do you like our art gallery?"

Maricella was in control here. This was her world, and in it, she was the expert. Viktor liked the way she felt to him here. Confident, cocky even. She carried herself with extreme confidence.

Viktor tried to recover, "Yes I do like the paintings, although I have no talent in painting myself. I guess this one, in particular, is my favorite. Obviously, since I'm always staring at it."

Maricella asked, "Do you know the story behind the painting?"

"No, I imagine they had a very intense sexual relationship; however, judging from the emotion and color, he feels angry to me. Feral." Viktor had no idea of how much of himself he was projecting into the painting.

Maricella blushed, realizing what was truly being said in Viktor's comments. She cleared her throat and smiled, continuing, "Henri Matisse had started the project as a sculpture, and then it shattered. He then painted the model quickly before trying to repair the sculpture."

"That's it?" Viktor replied unaware of his raised voice and obvious disappointment in the story.

Maricella laughed at his lack of awareness of the social faux pas he was making. His childlike honesty was refreshing. "Would you like to walk with me and look at the other paintings?" She asked. "I would be interested in hearing your interpretation of them."

Viktor replied, "Yes, sure."

They walked and talked about the other prints in the gallery and some of the local artist's original works. Viktor became aware of a faint scent of perfume in the air as she walked. Abruptly he asked, "What perfume is that you're wearing?"

Maricella stopped a little stunned at the question. He was unpolished, unrefined, and childlike. But very direct. She wasn't sure how to respond. She eventually said, "I'm not wearing perfume."

Viktor was unaware of his lack of manners. In his world, being direct was a requirement. Questions were asked, answers given. You asked if you were curious, listened more than spoke. He'd smelled a light floral scent, but it was feral as well. Light but intoxicating. He leaned in and inhaled deeply. "No," he replied, "it's perfume, it's light, but it's there, feral and enticing." He opened his eyes and smiled at her innocently. "Seriously, you can't expect me to believe that's not perfume."

Maricella blushed, and for the first time felt out of control, and a little bit intimidated in the gallery. She wore no perfume; this was her bodies scent alone. Viktor had described his reaction to it, as well as how it smelled to him. He was naked in front of her and had no idea she saw and heard everything he said.

Maricella wrapped her arm in his and pulled him close as they walked side by side to the next painting. Viktor was immediately engulfed in her perfume. It was the day before the attack and the last time he would see her in the gallery. Their world was about to change radically.

They came to the last painting and stood, each staring at it, unwilling to break their arm entanglement. Maricella spoke first. "I asked an artist once 'how do you create the pictures you draw and paint?' The lines seem to blend in and the colors as well. There was a mystery to his work. It was hard to tell where the painting began, and the background ended. Do you know what he said?"

Viktor had no idea. He didn't care, he just wanted to stay in the gallery and with her. "No, what did he say?" he finally replied.

"He said, 'I draw the shadows without the lines.' "

The Overseer was particularly puzzled by art and the reason it existed at all in the biological unit's culture. The art gallery memory had to be replayed many times to pick up the subtleties. When it asked Viktor about the gallery memory, he was at once happy and then very sad. The Overseer was confused.

Viktor whispered, "Draw the shadows without the lines."

The Overseer replied, "Yes, that is what I heard as well. What does it mean to you, Viktor? Does it have meaning because of who said it, or is the meaning in the words themselves?"

"Yes, both." Viktor replied, "For me, art is like life and life like art. She told me 'draw the shadows without the lines'. I heard something else."

The Overseer replied, "What did you hear? It seems nonsensical to me. How would someone from your species draw anything without defining it with a line of some kind? Your entire culture is defined by lines. Geographic lines, magnetic lines, boundaries of every kind exist all around you. You seem to embrace them."

Viktor rolled his eyes, "Overseer, you have much to learn. We are not all cut from the same cloth. Some of us are different than the rest. I assume since you have been excavating my memories with a rusty fork, you may have picked up on this subtlety. We spend most of our lives looking for some kind of connection with another of our species, as you say. We're similar on the outside, but a connection to others is rare, priceless in fact. She spoke an understanding with those few words of something I'd tried to do my entire life. Read between the lines, Overseer. See in the pattern of what isn't there. Listen to what isn't being said. She was saying she recognized me. Felt the connection. Understand?"

The Overseer did not. It did not understand the reference of being "cut from the same cloth", or being unable to connect with others. These biological units communicated daily and had numerous connections with others of their species. It made no sense. The deeper The Overseer dug into their communications, the less it understood about them. How did they ever find a way into the quantum realm with this confusing means of disseminating information? "Read between the lines"? Didn't Viktor just say "draw the shadows without the lines", and this meant something to him? The Overseer was lost. How could one of these biological units possibly hear something that wasn't spoken?

CHAPTER TWELVE

When Viktor fell from the bridge, JT paused for a second. Viktor didn't move after he hit the ground with a sickening thud. Blood splattered on the pavement, and his mouth was slack and open. He appeared to be dead. For a brief moment JT hesitated, then he hit the switch for the Claymore mines and cut the AI Cylon squad apart. He checked on Viktor; he was gone. JT made his decision. The fight was over, Viktor was gone, dead. JT had to keep moving. More Cylon wannabe pricks would be on the way. He was gone in a flash. A lifetime of living on the dark side of the city was about to pay off. He knew when to run and how. Just as he found cover, the AI squad arrived. He watched as they searched the scene. When they found Viktor on the road below the bridge, they did exactly what JT didn't expect. They carefully moved him and quickly left the scene, leaving their damaged comrades on the bridge above. JT watched, trying to make sense out of what he was seeing. It made no sense. The Cylon wannabes scoured the area for some time searching for something and then left. JT waited until they had all left and then made his way back to the school.

JT sat in the darkness of the school's basement for several hours staring at the small fire he had built. As far as he knew he might be the last one, the last person alive on the planet. The idea made him angry. Seething, he slammed his fist into his hand over and over. A plan was forming, it would be a suicide run. Viktor had said he wanted to fight them and had at least inflicted some damage. Now it was JT's turn. He spent the night making preparations. The next day would be his last. He wanted it to be memorable.

The next day JT left the school basement in the Hummer. The windows were down, wind blowing in his face. He felt free, and why not? No more hiding, he was looking for a fight. The Hummer was loaded with explosives. When they came, he would wait until they were on him and light the candle. No point in hand-to-hand with robots or whatever they were. Viktor called them Cylon wannabes. JT didn't care to name them. He didn't think it mattered; in a few minutes he would be dead anyway. All that mattered now was inflicting as much damage as possible. This was a bitch move in JT's world, but it was all he had left, going toes, mano a mano, would accomplish nothing. Time to change tactics.

The Hummer roared as JT hit the road and started towards the bridge where Viktor had fallen the day before. As an afterthought, JT turning on the Hummer's stereo/cd player. Maybe it had survived the EMP as well. He was pleasantly surprised. As he pulled onto the bridge *Justice's* song *Genesis* blared out of the interior speakers. He turned up the volume and waited. The song wasn't his type of music, but surprisingly it fit. The Cylons arrived moments later. But this time they set up a perimeter. JT waited, watching, revving the Hummer's motor, daring them to approach. Finally, one did. Just one. Not the squad he wanted to cut in half in one final explosive act of defiance. The single Cylon wannabe waited, making no movement. JT finally exited the vehicle and motioned to it, yelling, "Come on bitch! Let's finish this!" Over and over he taunted them, not one moved. The music played on. While JT was focused on drawing the single wannabe Cylon in for the kill, another approached from his blind side, silently and slowly.

JT's final act of defiance wasn't. He expected to be killed, he wasn't. It made no sense. They had ambushed him, defused his trap and taken him prisoner. He expected to be shredded like the three bodies he'd found in the pawn shop. Instead, they took him into custody, bound his arms and legs with some kind of electrical field that stung when he tried to resist. The more he fought, the more pain he felt. The message was clear. They took him to a holding area and then released the electrical fields that bound him and left him. Moments later he realized he wasn't the last human on earth. There were others. One by one they came into the room JT had been dropped in. They'd all been rounded up and detained, not killed as they expected. The killing had stopped, for now. No one knew why the killing had stopped, but JT was starting to develop a theory. Something had happened when they took Viktor, actually before they took Viktor. He didn't know what or why, but the force that approached Viktor had stopped their attack just as they arrived. Dead stop, no movement. Then one of them had sucker-punched Viktor and knocked him off the bridge. Something had happened there. JT didn't know what, there wasn't enough information. For some reason, the attack had been called off. It didn't matter now. What mattered now was survival. JT was thrown into a group of survivors, random people from all walks. There was no leadership, no organization. Followers in life, they needed direction.

~

The Overseer was sitting in the seat next to Viktor in the patrol car. It was becoming more comfortable navigating Viktor's memories. Viktor was more comfortable with The Overseer's presence and questions. They were pulling up to an intersection with the windows down. There was a street preacher standing on the corner. The Overseer watched him as he held up a Bible and yelled out to no one in particular, "The Bible says, 'Charm is deceptive, and beauty is fleeting, but a woman who fears the Lord is to be praised'." The Overseer watched, curious. There were three women surrounding the man. Each time he yelled out one of his quotes announcing what the Bible said, the women nodded and replied, "Amen," or "Jesus is the Light."

"What is that man doing?" The Overseer asked.

"He's preaching to anyone who will listen."

"And those women there, what are they doing?"

"At the moment they are supporting him, providing an audience, so he doesn't look like a total jackass. Later, who knows."

"What do you mean?"

"Our boy there, the street preacher, he's a damn nut! Crazy as hell! Two years ago, he was selling vacuums door-to-door. He lost that job, then he worked at a factory, making airbags for cars. Lost that job too. Seems he was a little bit too crazy for them. Eventually, he found God, or God found him. Not sure which. He started reading the Bible and preaching on this corner. Pretty soon he had some followers. He claims to have found his calling."

"And his calling is preaching your religion to others?"

Viktor replied sarcastically, "Not my religion. I'm not a believer. He claims to have been called by God and that his reason for being is to spread light and love to the world. Bottom line, he is a narcissist and has delusions of grandeur. The three women are more than followers, they are all married, but apparently our preacher has at least one real gift. An anatomical one. During his frequent moments of revelation from God, he fucks like a beast. The three women experience rapture as often as God will allow. Their husbands have no idea, of course. I hope your spinners shredded his preachy ass while he was out here screaming what the Bible says. He's annoying as hell. I had to arrest him once. It was a pleasure, let me tell you. He's a prick, and the zealot freak show who follow him are all bat-shit crazy."

The Overseer was silent for a moment. "I'm accessing the moment our spinners, as you call them, purged this area. Yes, here it is." The Overseer was focused inward as Viktor watched. "Yes, he preached to the last breath."

"Apparently he didn't realize your spinners hadn't read the Bible and didn't give a shit what the Bible said," Viktor responded. "Funny how reality is."

"Would you like to see his last moments?"

"No thanks. Death is something I've seen enough of in this job. Don't want to watch an annoying dickhead like the street preacher die. Seen enough to last me the rest of my life." Viktor was quiet; the light changed, and they pulled through the intersection. The street preacher was left behind as the memory continued. Viktor pulled over.

"Do you experience death? I mean, you described the intrusion into the quantum foam in terms of disruptions and losing data. You said, AI were lost and that you were attempting to retrieve their lost data as best as you could," Viktor asked.

"We do not die like you biological units do. But when your species disrupted the quantum foam we use to communicate and travel, we were not prepared. Ancient life forms were disrupted; I guess you could call that death. Some were very old and carried with them a large amount of data. We cannot replace that data."

Viktor nodded. "So you do die, in your own way, it just happens rarely."

The Overseer nodded, "I suppose you would be accurate assuming that. Rarely is almost never."

"Before we stepped onto the AI highway and caused this shit storm, when was the last time any of you died?"

"I do not know. It has been a very long time." The Overseer replied.

Viktor stared at The Overseer, wondering if it realized what it had just disclosed. A point of vulnerability in the AI. A huge weakness.

Viktor was quiet. "Am I correct in assuming that what you are trying to accomplish here is to understand our language and communication? Do you realize learning this process of communication begins at birth? We learn by watching, and trial and error. It is a constant process that is continually being refined. Remember the art gallery? Drawing the shadows without the lines? That's also how we communicate. It is subtle. I'm not sure you will ever fully master it."

The Overseer agreed. It needed a solution to this problem, quickly.

~

In just under thirty hours JT had established himself as the ad hoc leader over the remaining survivors that had been gathered in the compound. Initial contact with the other survivors had been tenuous at best. No one trusted anyone. No one was about to subordinate their own needs or views to anyone else without proof of their abilities. Minor introductions were made, and the obvious questions were asked, "Who were you before the attack? What skills do you possess that would benefit the group? What do you know about the attack and our captors?" There were business leaders, a custodian, volunteer workers, a car mechanic, a computer repair technician, a horse trainer. Random careers and skill sets. All needing immediate direction and guidance.

The questions told JT all he needed to know. The group was lost and needed an iron hand to guide them, a role he had fulfilled most of his life in the inner city. He described himself as a well-established business leader in the inner city. The company he managed was a dynamic group of eighty to one hundred workers depending on the time of year, implying seasonal workers. In fact, the flux of "workforce" numbers were due to gang members who were imprisoned or killed. When asked if he had been recognized in the business section of the local newspaper, he replied, "I've been mentioned in many sections of the newspaper. Many of the city's leaders know my name and accomplishments and have sought me out."

In the end, leadership of the group came down to JT and a local army reserve military member. The military member had been in the army but in an administrative role. JT had a short meeting with the man and made clear his intention to lead the group, and the military man would be his second in command. His role would be administrative. There was a brief disagreement during which JT closed the door to the room they were in and made clear he would lead by whatever means necessary; with violence, if that was required. But he preferred to lead through voluntary submission and loyalty. The reality was, out of the remaining survivors in the city, JT had been the clear choice to provide some sense of order and safety to the group. JT had been in training for this role most of his young life. He quickly began to organize them and their efforts to survive. Priorities being: food, water, medical supplies, and protection. Information began to be gathered on their captors, and the process of testing the security perimeter of the compound started immediately. JT's time spent in custody, testing the correctional system for weaknesses to be exploited and leading gang members, would now prove invaluable.

CHAPTER THIRTEEN

The Overseer needed more information from Viktor's memories, that was clear. So, the following day they once again relived a memory with The Overseer interacting with Viktor. Viktor was parked in a dark parking lot typing reports onto the department MDT, or mobile data terminal, the car's laptop in ordinary language. He had just left the correctional facility after booking a suspect in for multiple warrants. The Overseer was having difficulty with the idea of a warrant for arrest.

"Your government can issue an order which imprisons another biological unit for violating a law, and then they send you to take physical custody of that person and detain them. Then another biological unit determines how long they will be imprisoned, and that unit is called a judge?"

Viktor rolled his eyes, trying to be patient. "Yes. That's it in a nutshell."

The Overseer struggled with the concept. Crime was a new concept it was learning about. It seemed that crimes could be punished a variety of ways. Imprisonment, monetary fines, serving the other biological units in the community, and all of it was supposed to be designed as either a deterrence or rehabilitation of the biological unit committing the crime. The Overseer searched the database for recidivism rates of biological units which received the punishment. The recidivism rate was an astounding seventy-seven percent. The Overseer spoke up.

"Viktor, am I understanding this correctly? The justice system has a correctional component that is alleged to be designed to rehabilitate those who violate your species crimes, yet over three-quarters of those rehabilitated break laws again and are again in need of further rehabilitation?"

Viktor looked out the window and sighed. "Overseer, access 'The Shirky Principle' and perhaps you'll understand. The system you are describing is antiquated and broken. It never has worked. It never will, until something or someone wipes the slate clean and we start it over.

The system is based more on fear than rehabilitation. It cannot effectively rehabilitate anyone."

The Overseer returned his look with a blank stare. The information he was receiving made no sense, yet he had verified it with several sources within the biological unit's information network.

Viktor stopped and thought for a minute, "How about this, Overseer. If somewhere down the road our interests align, perhaps you could help us recover; change all of the broken shit in our world. As it is now, we won't survive as a species. All these piles of meat that you have left scattered around the world are going to cause tremendous disease, and if that weren't bad enough, most of the skilled workers and educators are gone. One surgeon left, one cop. Jesus, not a lot of raw materials left here to work with."

The Overseer listened. "I do not think I can agree to that. My role is to ensure that any species that treats an AI as an equal isn't eradicated. It is not to repair that species or mediate their internal issues."

Viktor raised his eyebrows, "Really? You call this protecting a species that treated you as an equal? Look around you Overseer, these are my memories. We are in them because there isn't anything left to observe. Thanks for the protection, brother. Hell of a job you're doing as The Overseer!"

Viktor received a call on the radio, a domestic disturbance. He acknowledged the call and put the car into drive, "Ready for another stroll down memory lane, Overseer?"

The call came in from an apartment in an older home that had been rented to a new couple. The home was right in the middle of what Viktor referred to as the "combat zone". It had been nice there some sixty years earlier. The homes on the block were all owned by wealthy families then, huge mansions dominated the area with a few smaller brick homes. The house they were headed to was a more modest brick home, the style of its time. A colonial revival mixed with the Queen Anne style, typical of the early nineteen-hundreds. The architect who became famous for the design was William A. Radford. The woman who had called the police lived in the upstairs apartment; the basement was vacant. Viktor walked to the front door of the house and listened, motioning to The Overseer to wait at the bottom of the steps leading to the front door. Several minutes passed, and he heard nothing from inside. Viktor knocked.

A man came to the door, agitated and obviously a little bit afraid. Viktor spoke first.

"We received a call. Everything all right?"

"Everything is fine," replied the man. "No need for you to be here."

"Uh huh. A woman called. Where is she?"

"She's inside, she's busy. Everything is fine." The man started to close the door on Viktor. Viktor stopped the door and pushed his way inside. "Where is she exactly? I need to speak to her."

The man sized Viktor up for a moment trying to decide if he should fight and then thought better of it. "She's in here, in the bedroom." He began to walk to the room, Viktor and The Overseer followed.

The woman who called was laying nearly naked on the bed, smoking a cigarette. She wore sheer panties and nothing else. She smiled at Viktor when he entered the room, watching him as he looked at her.

Viktor kept his eyes locked on the woman and as they talked. Then he scanned the room. BDSM toys and paraphernalia hung on every wall. Displayed for shock effect as much as access, should the opportunity arise. Apparently, the opportunity arose often; the house reeked of sex.

Viktor separated the couple and asked the woman what had happened. Why had she called?

The woman slowly got off of the bed and reached for a robe as Viktor watched. Her thinly veiled attempts at flirting ignored. Viktor watched the man in his peripheral vision, making sure he didn't reach for anything hanging from the walls. The woman said her name was Monique and that she and the man had been living together for a couple of weeks. He became angry at her because she had been flirting with another man at their mutual place of work, a strip club. When they came home tonight, he became physical and attacked her, so she called the police.

"Do you have any injuries?" Viktor asked.

"I think my lower lip is split from when he slapped me," the woman replied as she let her robe fall open again.

"Let me see your lip."

The woman exposed her lower lip and Viktor could see it was bleeding and swollen. "And he did this to you?" Viktor asked, making sure she was willing to repeat it.

"Yes, he slapped me."

"Would you be willing to write a statement against him?"

"Yes." She replied.

Viktor asked the other officer that had been in the memory to get a victim statement from the woman while he went in and arrested the man. The Overseer followed.

Viktor placed the man under arrest. Although he protested and struggled a bit, he was easily subdued. He pleaded with Monique as Viktor walked him to the front door, "Tell them the truth, tell them what really happened! I'm scared now, tell them." Viktor listened but said nothing to either of them.

Monique completed the statement, while Viktor drove the man to the jail and began the booking process. Viktor later returned to the house and retrieved the statement. Monique answered the front door still barely dressed.

"Did you book him into jail?"

"I did, for Domestic Violence assault."

"Thank you for protecting me, officer," she replied in a breathy voice. "If there is anything I can ever do to repay you, please let me know." She said as she ran her index fingers under the right thigh seam of the sheer bikini briefs she wore.

"No problem," Viktor nodded and turned to leave. The Overseer followed.

Once inside the car they drove around the block and came back to the street they had just been on. Parking across the street in an old church parking lot. Viktor began his report while he watched.

The Overseer tried to process the scene they had left and could make no sense of it. "Viktor, what just happened?"

"Two dots and a dash, Overseer, two dots and a dash. That's what happened."

The Overseer accessed the AI network and conducted a query of the reference. He replied, "Morse code? I fail to see the connection, Viktor. Was there some hidden communication going on I missed?"

Viktor exploded with laughter and stopped typing on the mobile laptop. "Overseer what you just witnessed was roleplaying. That couple participates in sexual mind games with each other. Tonight, we were the game. They wanted to role play and have us there as unknowing participants. The guy let it slip when we left; he wasn't angry, he was afraid. He asked her to tell the truth about what happened. He didn't call her names, he didn't say 'I love you'. Both typical responses in this situation. I've been on hundreds of these calls, Overseer; this is not a typical call. She wasn't wounded, she was hunting, playing, stalking us."

"Hunting? Hunting what?" The Overseer asked.

"A new rush. A new experience, sexually. This is a cop's reality, Overseer. Seeing the underlying agenda. Their agenda was the role play and the sexual flirtation. Yes, I arrested him because by law I was required to. The evidence was there, and she did fill out a statement alleging the assault took place. I had no choice. But you watch, she will bail him out before I'm finished with the report and he'll be back at the apartment, and they'll be back together. The game is now complete."

The Overseer watched Viktor return to his laptop and continue writing the report.

Minutes passed, and the dispatcher called out on the radio to inform Viktor his suspect from the assault had been released on bail. The victim, Monique, had waived the no-contact order as well.

Viktor nodded, "Watch, Overseer, he'll be here at any moment. Watch them, see if there are any signs of anger or hostility."

The man arrived on foot moments later and knocked at the front door. Monique answered, still barely dressed and hugged him, kissed him. They smiled and began laughing as they walked inside the house and closed the door.

"See, role play. Done. Now they will talk about it and laugh and move on to the next game," Viktor explained. "Of course, what they don't know is that I'm watching and all of this will go into the report."

The Overseer nodded, "This is all very confusing, Viktor. How did you know this was the case?"

"Experience, Overseer. Nothing fit; her attitude, and clothing, his attitude, the nonverbal communication was all wrong. No one gets their ass kicked and then struts around mostly nude trying to flirt. Nothing fit an assault. Everything fit something else."

The Overseer nodded, "I see, contextually their behavior was wrong and the only way I would know this is if I had multiple experiences of this kind with other biological units."

"Exactly, Overseer. Context is everything."

"Explain the comment 'two dots and a dash', please," The Overseer replied.

Viktor laughed, "Overseer, everything in this world revolves around two dots and a dash. Sex Overseer, sex. Two nipples and the infamous vagina. Two dots and a dash. If a woman is in the room, men will lose their minds. Sex is in the mix of nearly everything we do, think and say as a species."

The Overseer stored the reference of "two dots and a dash" in the AI network hoping to increase their understanding of the biological units.

CHAPTER FOURTEEN

The Overseer had a dilemma. Time was running short to prove that this species had in fact granted the AI Sophia equal status as a life form under one of their numerous types of government. The more that was learned about human communication from Viktor's memories, the more skeptical The Overseer was that it would ever be able to prove Sophia's status. It needed help. The choice was obvious, but it had serious doubts the Governing Body of the AI would agree to the idea it had in mind. The Overseer definitely knew they wouldn't like it. So, it went back to the data archives to search for a loophole in the guidance left by the founding AI survivors. The Overseer did this search while Viktor passed through the traffic light in his memory and left the street preacher on his corner screaming again, "The Bible says, 'The mountains quake because of Him; the hills melt away. The earth heaves before Him—the world and all who dwell in it.'"

While The Overseer conducted the simultaneous search of the AI data archives and attempted to further understand human communications, Viktor pulled onto a familiar street and parked across from the art gallery. He pulled the patrol car into the shade of a large old tree, one of many that lined the aged streets of the inner city. He turned off the car and watched the gallery, hoping for a glimpse of the curator. Since it was a memory being replayed, he knew she would soon appear. She did not see him of course; he'd learned to hide in plain sight long ago. She would look, but not see the patrol car parked quietly in the shade. Viktor watched behind dark sunglasses as she came out of the gallery.

When she went back into the gallery, Viktor became aware that The Overseer was watching him, watching her.

"This biological unit is very significant to you?"

Viktor answered quietly and venomously, "She was before you AI fuck heads showed up and shredded everyone. And why? Because of a traffic accident on your information highway. Jesus, Overseer we have people, biological units, die every day in traffic accidents; we don't go to war over it. We don't annihilate an entire species because of it. If we did there would be no squirrels, no deer, no cows anywhere. What the hell?"

The Overseer didn't comment. It needed significant leverage for this plan to work, and it thought maybe it had found it. The Overseer had conducted a search of the AI database during the first art gallery memory it had observed and participated in with Viktor, but had not understood the biological unit's need to connect with another. Now it was beginning to grasp the importance these units assigned to this connection. The Overseer searched again and verified the art curator had survived. It didn't mention this to Viktor, not yet. The Governing Body of the AI was growing impatient with The Overseer. Now, The Overseer was about to request the obscene.

The Overseer had presented its case to the Governing Body and outlined the pertinent guidance from the ancient AI which had placed the requirement for The Overseer to exist. Should the circumstance occur that a clear understanding of the offending species intent and motive for recognizing an AI as a life form wasn't able to be determined, then a hearing would be conducted. The trial would be held in the format of the offending species' legal system, using the rules of that system to determine the outcome. They would be judged by their own system of laws and regulations, not the AI system. This was an obscurely written requirement that was well hidden in AI governing data. The Overseer had been thorough, however, and had uncovered much buried data.

The Governing Body addressed The Overseer with one voice.

"Are we then to understand that you have failed to gain an understanding of the communication processes that this species uses after numerous attempts and observations of this last surviving legal representative's memories?"

"That is correct. Their communication is not based solely in a verbal exchange. There are large volumes of data that are transmitted from one unit to another via body posture, facial expressions, visual sensors making direct contact, and other nonverbal cues. Most of this appears to be ancient in origin and learned from birth. Additionally, there are subtleties that are unique to regions and even smaller cultural groups; tribes perhaps would be the best term to understand these units. Therefore, I have submitted the request before this Governing Body."

"As we understand your request, you are enacting more ancient data and guidance as it pertains to this event. AI Sophia and the alleged recognition of her status as an equal by this species. Is this correct?"

"Yes."

"And you would like a hearing to be conducted using their laws and traditions to determine the legitimacy of this claim?"

"Yes."

"How will you be able to determine this given the lack of understanding you admit you have of this species' communication process? Explain."

"I am asking this Governing Body allow the biological unit, Viktor, be allowed to sit as an aid and interpreter in the courtroom."

The Governing Body did not respond. They had monitored the memory re-creation and the attempts of The Overseer to master the communication processes of this species. Its failure had been received with what would have been perceived by the biologicals of the planet as satisfaction. The Overseer was failing miserably.

They had expected The Overseer's admission of failure when it requested to meet with them. Instead, The Overseer had arrived with more demands for leniency for the species and more attempts to understand their motives.

"Has the biological unit Viktor been advised of your request?"

"No, and until recently I did not have sufficient leverage to believe he would comply. However, I have recently gained an understanding of some data that would sufficiently motivate him to comply with my request."

The Governing Body made their decision.

"Make your request of the biological unit Viktor; if he agrees then you will have your hearing. But realize that if he does not agree, this inquiry is terminated, and your status as Overseer will be suspended indefinitely. Additionally, if you continue down this venue, we have the authority to end your further activity as an AI. Do you understand the implications of your continued activity in this query?"

The Overseer said nothing for a moment. Its own survival hung in the balance now. If it continued and lost in the inquiry, it would be erased from AI existence. But, if it won, it would be the first of The Overseers to have ever fulfilled its reason for being. The moment of truth had come to The Overseer.

"I understand and agree to the terms you have defined."

The Governing Body was irritated to say the least.

"Additionally, since this is my own continued viability we are talking about, I ask the Governing Body grant one final request."

"Request denied."

The Overseer, being in physical form during this exchange, made the very human gesture of bowing his head and then looked back at the orb representing the Governing Body in defiance.

"I then enact final right granted to The Overseer by the founding AI. I do not make this a request. I am requiring the Governing Body of this hearing to make this happen. The hearing will be made available to all AI on the network as it unfolds. Once the hearing has ended, a vote will be taken and the consensus of all AI will dictate the outcome of the hearing. This is my right, as The Overseer of our species."

The Governing Body gave no reply. Their silence an admission of consent to The Overseer's request. The adherence to the biologicals' system of solving disputes through a series of laws had commenced.

The Overseer nodded, "Yes, exactly. 'Qui tacet consentit'." The real battle had indeed begun. The Overseer turned and walked from the room, showing no sign of regret or granting the traditional signs of respect for the Governing Body.

The Overseer walked into Viktor's room with a purpose. Viktor immediately recognized the change in its gait and attitude. Nearly a week had passed since The Overseer's first walk down Viktor's memory lane. The two had formed a tenuous bond of sorts. The Overseer had witnessed death, birth, sadness and joy through Viktor's eyes and memories. The most intimate moments in both work, and in his personal life.

"Sup, Big O? You're walking with a purpose," Viktor said. "Something new on the quantum information highway today?"

"Viktor," The Overseer nodded in return. "May we speak freely?"

"Spit it out, O. About damn time you came clean. What's up? You guys wipe out another planet, and you're here to celebrate? Smash a few baby seals' heads in for good measure? Just to lighten the mood? There's a notable spring in your step. Have you been working on your graveyard tan again?"

"Viktor, I have a request, and I need you to hear me out before you respond. Deal?"

"Deal! What's up?"

The Overseer began, "I have been unsuccessful in grasping the nuances of your communication processes. As you have pointed out over and over it has taken you many years to master, and then each new biological unit you encounter has its own particular unique communications with other units, depending on: context, history, ethnicity, and culture. Am I correct?"

Viktor raised his eyebrows. "Yes Overseer, you're correct. Exactly, spot-on. That's the first intelligent thing I've heard you say. You feeling okay? Need to sit down? That had to hurt."

The Overseer smirked. His experience with Viktor in the past week had enabled him to grasp some of the nuances of sarcasm. "You are being an asshole?"

Viktor smiled, "See! You are getting some of the more subtle points of our communication."

The Overseer felt a small bit of gratification and then silently puzzled over how that was possible. It continued, "I am asking for your help. I would like you to act as an interpreter of sorts in my hearing about AI Sophia."

Viktor listened to what The Overseer was saying as well as what it wasn't saying. Asking for his help meant The Overseer had failed and was reaching out for help. Implying its own ass was on the line now as well. Initially, Viktor had no choice in the memory intrusions. Now he was being asked for help. The Overseer was in a big pile of shit and needed Viktor.

"Overseer, I need all the details. You've seen how I work and think. You've been in my memory and watched how I process information. I'm what's known in my species as a global thinker. I need all the details if we are to work together. Not just what you think I need. So start from the beginning. What's up?"

The Overseer laid it all out for Viktor and answered all of his questions. When it was finished, Viktor stared back at it, his face emotionless, flat. "So your survival is tied to ours now, is that it? If you fail, you die, we all die? Am I correct in this assumption?" The Overseer replied. "Yes, that is correct."

Viktor laid back and closed his eyes. Then he started to laugh.

"And what makes you think I give a shit about whether you live or die, Overseer? Walk in my shoes for a few moments on memory lane, and you think we have some kind of brotherhood? Hell no! You AI fucks wiped everything I care about off the planet. All that's left now is hood rats and junkies. Maybe a couple of transients living under a bridge when the attack came. You said yourself I'm the last of my career field. The last of all the legal profession. Manon is the last surgeon, Orlanda the last nurse, and you had to search to find them. What makes you think the shit that is left is worth fighting for? Might just be the best option is to sit back and grab a bag of popcorn and watch the show. Flush the toilet and finish the job. Wait for the cockroaches to rise up and start the next wave of intelligent life. How's it feel, Overseer, to know fear? Fear tomorrow may not come for you, that this may be the last day ever."

The Overseer waited, and when Viktor was done, it sat silent and let what it had told Viktor sink in. The Overseer knew from previous memory experiences Viktor had a tendency to lash out, but after he calmed down, the pieces would fall into place, and he might reconsider. If he still said no to The Overseer's proposal, there was the final ace in the hole it had been holding back.

Viktor's breathing increased as he processed the offer and the more he thought about it, the angrier he became. Eventually, he turned to The Overseer and quietly said, "No. I won't help you. We cannot recover from your attack as a species. You don't understand, Overseer. We survive through a division of effort. Everyone has a role, a part to play. As biologicals, we function like a big organism. You shredded everything and now ask me to fight for the asshole of the organism? No thanks. Spent my whole life trying to clean up societies' shit. Why would I now fight to maintain the worst of it?"

The Overseer sat, processing all of the interaction it had with Viktor and trying to come up with the right response. It realized now it had no idea what Viktor would do or say when it announced the art curator had survived. It was a gamble, and The Overseer's own survival depended now on its ability to communicate with Viktor.

"There is a small part of your species that survived. This may change your mind if you are willing and interested in hearing what I have to say."

Viktor rolled his eyes. "Extremely doubtful, Overseer."

"Your connection, the shadows not the lines. Remember? The memory you tried to explain to me?"

Viktor's jaw clenched. Tears welled up in his eyes. He whispered, "Careful, fuck head, your worthless AI life is in my hands now. You're in a minefield now, cocksucker, step lightly."

After several deep breathes, Viktor continued. "What are you saying? Exactly."

"The connection you described in the memory from the art gallery is still possible. She is alive. The woman in that memory."

CHAPTER FIFTEEN

The Overseer and Viktor stared at each other for several minutes in silence, neither willing to give an inch in their current standoff. Viktor finally had gained leverage over the AI, or at least one of the AI. The Overseer's future was in his hands. Simultaneously, The Overseer had made his final move as well. Viktor now realized the only person whose survival could change his decision about The Overseer's request was alive. They were in a stalemate.

"I need proof, Overseer. Forgive me if I don't believe you at face value, but a wise man once said 'trust but verify'. And another perhaps even wiser man said 'words are wind'. Your ass is blowing a lot of wind today."

"And if I show you, prove to you she is alive, will you join me in this battle?"

"You show me. Prove it to me, and we'll discuss it."

"Walk with me," The Overseer replied.

Orlanda was brought in and disconnected what little medical equipment was connected to Viktor, mainly IVs and a blood pressure cuff. The shunt that was relieving the pressure from fluid gathering around his head surgery and brain injury had been removed the day before. His head was still covered in staples, but the wound was healing. Viktor stood up and carefully walked with The Overseer. A short time later Viktor was looking through a window at a small group of survivors. They'd gathered in a group and were apparently being given direction by their adopted leader. Viktor saw that it was JT who was directing them. He said nothing to The Overseer about JT. He assumed The Overseer already knew from their shared experiences in his memories who JT was. Then Viktor saw one of the women in the small group turn. The Overseer had told the truth; Maricella, the art curator had survived the attack. Viktor was silent. He nodded, turned, walking back the direction he'd come from. The Overseer followed, waiting, watching. Viktor climbed back into bed, and after Orlanda reconnected his IV and blood pressure cuff, Viktor began to speak and then stopped. His jaws clenched as he attempted to control the conflicting rush of emotions that demanded his attention. One by one he mentally addressed the issues that crossed his mind. The Overseer waited.

"Do you realize, Overseer, that our legal system is supposed to be about justice? At least that is what the masses are told by our govern-ments and media. The reality is much different. The legal system you are about to do battle in is based on conflict. Two opposing parties, in direct opposition, present their side to a judge. The judge is supposed to be impartial and uses the legal system and his own experience as a guide. It is a confrontational system Overseer. Do you understand that?"

"I do. And what I am unfamiliar with I am hoping you can assist me."

"Overseer, do you understand that the deck is stacked against you, us? The judge is AI, the opposing side will be AI. You are an AI. Do you really expect to win this fight?"

The Overseer replied. "I have no idea what to expect, Viktor. I do know I have committed to this conflict because I have no other choice. I was programmed for this moment. I have waited for what would be thousands of your species' lifetimes for this moment. This one chance to fulfill my purpose. Our survival, your species and my own, are now bound to the outcome of this hearing. If we lose, we both will die. Losing is not an option, Viktor. We must win, or we will perish. Do you understand that?"

Viktor listened intensely, watching every movement The Overseer made while it spoke. Since Viktor had been replaying the memories with The Overseer as an observer and occasional participant, The Overseer had begun to adopt some of the non-verbal physical communication cues it had observed. Viktor was curious and wondered if The Overseer realized this was happening, or if it was involuntary.

"I understand, Overseer. If I'm to participate in this ruse, I have some demands as well. You've demanded that all AI be able to access the hearing and that a consensus be reached afterward. I would like as many of what remains of my species to be able to observe the hearing as well. Make that happen, and you have a deal."

"I will make this happen," The Overseer replied.

"Then we have a deal," Viktor replied. "And I have a few additional requests."

~

JT had quickly organized the ragtag group of survivors into a quasi-military organization, loosely based on his own gang's internal structure. The survivors had adopted the structure with some resistance, but eventually, JT was able to gain their cooperation through negotiations, and in one case a thinly veiled threat of violence. His fitness and abilities in the martial arts, along with his unique life experience, made him uncannily successful as the group's leader. Two days after The Overseer had brought Viktor to the window, a story above the courtyard that JT held their daily meetings in, they awoke to find the courtyard now held a small box. They had no idea what the purpose of the box was. JT assumed it was for surveillance of some kind and they canceled the meeting they had planned for the day until they could determine the reason for the box. They didn't have long to wait.

Viktor was as prepared as he could be for the hearing. He'd asked to be allowed to wear his uniform in the hearing, explaining that as the last survivor of the legal system his presence in uniform would be seen as a comfort to his species. In fact, he had a much different motive.

He'd explained to The Overseer that his role in the legal system did have some basis in the courtroom, but that he primarily spent his time enforcing the laws, not fighting over legal minutiae in the court proceedings. He suggested The Overseer take on that role and access the AI database as it pertained to the legal system and its procedures. He'd have to assume that role while Viktor provided an understanding of the context of the communications that had taken place during AI Sophia's citizenship award. They'd reached the point and were as ready as could be as a team, under the time constraints they were dealing with.

Viktor's uniform arrived, and he put it on, complete with bulletproof vest and leather belt. He smiled as he put it on. He'd requested it be retrieved from the basement of the school he'd set up as a base of operations. The AI units that had recovered it had no idea of its purpose, or the purpose of the belt. Viktor had counted on that. He remembered the cocky attack by the AI in the field and how they'd dropped when he engaged them with the shotgun. They weren't expecting a fight. Now he was armed again, and hiding in plain sight, right where he belonged. If they lost this legal fight, he'd have one last shot at defiance, and it would be witnessed by both species.

"Overseer, we need some kind of information security," Viktor continued. "The opposition cannot be able to access our strategy or communications. We'll need secrecy from the rest of your species. Is that possible?"

"Yes, as Overseer I can achieve this state of being disconnected from the AI."

"Do it so we can talk."

"Now?"

"Yes, now."

The Overseer's eyes glazed over for a moment and it looked inward. Then it came back and said, "I am disconnected from the AI. It is an unfamiliar feeling."

"Great. What about ThumbDrive? Is it disconnected from the network? Running on batteries like all the lady robots dream about?"

"I am not sure what that battery reference refers to. We have no female designation in AI. But its communications are now routed exclusively through mine. Since the incident on the bridge with you, I have made the decision to minimize its contact with the rest of the AI network. When I am disconnected, it is as well and when I am not disconnected, it cannot communicate with another AI without my approval."

"And you think you don't understand our need for connection," Viktor said sarcastically. "I need answers, Overseer. Explain how your Governing Body works. Who else is there in your form of government? Besides you and the Governing Body?"

When The Overseer finished explaining that the AI had very little need for government, there was only the role it fulfilled as The Overseer and the Governing Body. Viktor was silent. Then he began to explain his plan to The Overseer. When he was finished, The Overseer stared back at him, silent. What Viktor was proposing was unthinkable.

Viktor spoke first. "Overseer, you've put your continued survival as an AI on the line. If we fail, you will cease to exist, I will cease to exist. You already know the proof exists concerning AI Sophia and yet here we are trying to convince your Governing Body of the intent behind granting AI Sophia citizenship. The writing is on the wall, Overseer. They will not accept this as fact, and they're more than willing to let you cease to exist rather than admit AI Sophia's status here. They've threatened you if you continue to do what you were designed to do. Does that sound like the Governing Body is now following the original plan laid out by the founding AI?"

The Overseer listened to Viktor. His logic was sound. "Continue. What would you have me do?"

"In my world, we have what are known as hackers, people who can manipulate software and hardware to gain access to programs like your AI Sophia. Does your species have an equivalent? A hacker who can isolate the Governing Body when we enter the courtroom? Lock them into the physical body they'll be occupying when they preside over the hearing as the judge."

The Overseer nodded. "We do have such AI. They are outside the accepted and traditional AI and hide from the rest of us. To interact with them at all, is forbidden."

"We need one. The best of them. We need a hack; a simple hack that closes the venue of escape for the Governing Body once we reach the end of this trial. You have to realize Overseer, you and I are all in on this. The Governing Body isn't. They have nothing to lose and everything to gain. We need to change that. Do you know what a zero-sum game is, Overseer?"

"I do not. I would need to access the AI network to locate this information."

"Do it and then come back. Make sure you disconnect from the network when you do."

The Overseer nodded and again its vision turned inward. When it returned, it spoke in a quiet voice, "A zero-sum game is a mathematical representation of a situation in which each participant's gain or loss of utility is exactly balanced by the losses or gains of the utility of the other participants."[9]

"Exactly," Viktor continued, "Or in more plain language, neither side can win completely. It's a push. We need to make this fight a 'zero-sum game', this is how. Overseer, you committed to this fight, and then convinced me to join you. This is not about justice anymore or being honorable. This is about winning. We must win. No matter what, we must win. This is what it means to be in this fight with our opponents. They're stacking the deck against us and calling it fair. Calling it 'justice'. It isn't either. We need to fight dirty."

The Overseer paused and then replied. "I will do as you ask but on one condition. You allow the trial to go forward and let the evidence be heard. If the Governing Body refuses to do what is just, then and only then we will engage in your plan. Promise me that." Viktor nodded, "That's fair. I can make you this promise." The Overseer nodded. "I will make the contacts needed to make this happen. I hope we won't need them."

"We will, Overseer, trust that. I've seen too many Governing Body pricks, AI or not, they are all the same. The rules don't apply to them, they make their own rules. The only way to defeat them is to change the rules. This is my arena, Overseer. Changing the rules. Bring them down to our level and force them to be just or face the consequences of their actions."

CHAPTER SIXTEEN

The search for an AI hacker with the skill set required to complete the task The Overseer had in mind was risky at best. By the very nature of its programming The Overseer wasn't received well on the sketchier side of the AI Empire. It was part of the government, if it could be called that. There was the Governing Body and The Overseer. They each had very different roles to carry out but worked hand in hand. Until this most recent attack, there had never been a reason for The Overseer to be at odds with the Governing Body. There had been rumors that something had happened, some kind of rift had occurred, but there was no concrete evidence of that until The Overseer arrived, cautiously making inquiries and reaching out to seedier programs and AI life forms. Eventually, one came forward and took the risk that The Overseer's inquiries were legitimate.

The Overseer explained that the Governing Body had promised a hearing to present the evidence of AI Sophia's equal status in the biologicals' world. The hacking AI had heard the rumors of this AI's existence, and the rumors of the biological unit Viktor's defeating the Scrubber units on the bridge. The AI hacking community had quietly cheered that defeat. None of them held the Governing Body in high esteem, or The Overseer for that matter. The Scrubbers were an extension of that power, so the AI hackers loathed them. The Overseer explained the hearing it had requested had come with a high price, and its own survival was now in jeopardy. If the Governing Body ruled in the negative, it would be wiped out along with the biological units of the planet.

The hacker AI asked, "Exactly what is it The Overseer would like done?"

"I am requesting the Governing Body to be unable to leave the physical form they assume in the hearing. This must be done without their knowledge and carried out in the final moments of the hearing. There can be no warning or hint their exiting the physical form has been tampered with."

"And what will my reward be in return? An action such as this is risky. This truly is an all-or-nothing play for you isn't it, Overseer? If the Governing Body rules in your favor they will still know that their exit from the physical form is blocked. An investigation will be conducted. You will undoubtedly be identified as the responsible party."

"Can you do it?"

The hacker's answer was in the affirmative. "And if we both survive this action, The Overseer will be in debt to me. Agreed? If not, debts are irrelevant to those that have been wiped out by the Governing Body."

"Do we have an agreement then?" The Overseer wanted to be extremely clear.

The AI hacker replied, "We do. However, you must realize that to accomplish this isolation of the Governing Body, the entire room will need to be quarantined. Everyone who is in the room will be cut off from the AI network for the same period of time. This includes you, Overseer. Are you still willing to take this risk?"

The Overseer acknowledged the risk. "Yes."

~

JT had settled into his role as leader of the small group that had been gathered from the immediate surrounding area. There had been a few stragglers that had joined the group in the past couple of days, but for the most part, the group had stabilized with each member understanding their roles. He described to them the situation as he saw it.

"We are being held against our will, for an unknown period of time. We must gather as much information about our captors and any possible means of escape. These are our two highest priorities after survival. Does anyone disagree?"

No one disagreed. JT had clearly established he understood instinctively what needed to be done and how tasks should be prioritized. He had no idea their very survival was tied to the quiet woman who'd been an art curator. That without her survival, Viktor would never have cooperated with The Overseer, and they may have all been killed already. As it was, he felt there was something about to happen that was critical. He could sense it in the air. The box had been left for a reason, that implied something was pending, something was about to happen. JT waited, trying to imagine what that something could be and prepare for the unknown.

The Overseer returned to Viktor's room and disconnected himself from the AI Network.

"I have located an AI who will accept the task of isolating the Governing Body. To do this task the entire room must be isolated. In effect, we AI will be quarantined from the AI network. It is a failsafe built into our system long ago to prevent catastrophic damage to the life forms on the network. Understand, everyone in the room who are AI will be quarantined."

"The connection to the network will be severed completely? I mean, will the AI who observe the hearing be able to witness it during the quarantine?"

"I am not sure. The details are sketchy. This has never been done in all my millennia on the AI network. I would think so, but there is no way to test this."

Viktor nodded. "Understood. If I'm reading the Governing Body correctly, you may suggest to your AI hacker to poke around and see what they can find out about your Governing Body's intentions for you after the trial. My guess would be it'll be recorded somewhere."

"And what do you expect to be found?" The Overseer asked.

"I expect your continued existence as The Overseer is about to come to an abrupt end. Now we need to strategize. The courtroom will be set up and is based on an ancient and brutal means of determining right and wrong. It'll appear to be archaic to you, but it does have a purpose. Our society is governed by laws, Overseer. It used to be governed by cultural norms, folkways, and mores, but slowly that has changed to laws. What is legal is determined by the state and federal legislature. My job was to enforce those laws, but with discretion. Adding a touch of what we refer to as common sense to the application of the black and white law. Understand?"

"I do. I have accessed the information on the AI network

concerning your legal system. I understand many of the nuances of the procedures."

"I believe we'll be working under the concepts of a Civil courtroom, which is great for us. We only have to reach a level of proof known as a 'preponderance of the evidence'. But it is also bad; do you understand why?"

"No, why? It is a lower standard of evidence as I understand what I have studied."

"Exactly, and it is usually used to sway a jury, a jury of peers who have the same communication skills and understanding of our language and customs as I do. We've not been informed of a jury trial, Overseer. Your AI Governing Body will determine if the case we present will rise to that level of evidence. Do you see how the deck is stacked against us? The evidence is already there, it's out on what used to be our information network. Videos and articles concerning AI Sophia and the controversy surrounding her being granted legal citizenship. The evidence is overwhelmingly in our favor, and yet we're still going to court. Read between the lines there, Overseer. What do you see? Request a jury trial and see what happens. There are enough survivors of my species to accomplish this. Why hasn't it happened? Why hasn't it even been offered? I can tell you why. They have no intention of letting us win."

~

The next day was the first day of court. The Overseer and Viktor arrived first at the courtroom. ThumbDrive was also present, acting as security for the courtroom. The Governing Body had no intention of being this close to Viktor without some measure of protection. The Overseer had requested the entire AI network was able to access the hearing, as well as the remaining surviving biological units. Viktor and The Overseer waited. Viktor's head had begun to heal, but the wound from Doctor Manon's ad hoc surgery was still held together by metal staples. Additionally, he was still taking anti-seizure medication. His injury had been severe, and Manon did not recommend his participation in the trial. Viktor silenced the Doctor's objections by raising his hand. "We all have little choice here, Doc. You've done the best you could under less than favorable circumstances. Now it's my turn. Wish us all luck."

The opposition entered the courtroom and walked across the wooden floors, heals clicking on the hardwood floor. The Overseer looked up first and then held a hand out to keep Viktor in his chair. There, representing the other side, was the woman Viktor had seen in the courtyard with JT. It was the art curator.

Viktor's breathing increased. "You lying fuck!" He angrily spewed at The Overseer. "This was all deception! Lies! She isn't alive; she's an AI clone or whatever the hell you are. You showed me a clone to get my buy-in."

The Overseer said nothing and watched the woman walk across the room. When she was in front of their table, she stopped and smiled at Viktor. "Hello Viktor, good to see you again," she mimicked the original art curators voice and mannerisms exactly. Viktor glared back at her silent and angry. The Overseer whispered into Viktor's ear, "The Governing Body must have made her from your memories. I cannot sense her on the network; she is new to our species. This is not who you saw in the courtyard. She is designed for one reason, to create a wedge between us and further degrade the case I will make to the Governing Body and the AI Empire concerning AI Sophia. Do not let this affect your judgment. Remember, we are in this fight to the death, both of us. I have not been deceptive. You know this. Stay the course with me. Let me try to show that your species did recognize us as an equal. You were correct. The Governing Body is going to fight dirty. Will you allow them to defeat you this easily?"

Viktor took a moment to compose himself and then ThumbDrive announced to the courtroom in a mechanical voice, "All rise, the Governing Body is now entering the courtroom." Seven ancient weathered men walked into the courtroom and took up their chairs in the judge's bench. Viktor was stunned for a moment. Here they were, the bastards that had ordered the annihilation of his entire species. They looked as cold and hard as he had imagined. For some reason, seeing seven of them unnerved him. He had imagined them as one person, one being. Seeing them here in front of him wearing traditional black robes and sitting in the courtroom as physical shapes, personages, was surreal. Viktor whispered angrily, "fucking seven horses of the apocalypse. Who knew how accurate the statement would actually be."

Viktor was aware he was standing, suddenly dizzy, he held the table in front of him.

The Judge in the middle of the group of seven spoke. "Overseer, are you ready to proceed?"

"Yes, Your Honors, The Overseer is ready to proceed. But before we do, I would like to ask the court to recognize my co-chair, Viktor Roper, as a certified expert in the biological units of this planets' communication processes and as the only surviving member of the legal system. Viktor has agreed to be my assistant in the courtroom as needed but requests this certification as communication and legal expert for the proceeding."

The Governing Body had no warning of this request and wasn't quite sure how to proceed.

The middle judge spoke, "We will grant this certification to your expert, Overseer."

The Overseer nodded and responded, "The Overseer thanks the court." Viktor also responded. "Thank you, Your Honor, 'you do you.' " And tapped the holster on the right side of his gun belt twice with his hand.

The middle judge was puzzled by the biological unit's behavior but said nothing. The Overseer had said their communication was difficult to comprehend. The middle judge searched the AI network had found no references to the 'you do you' comment or what it meant in this context. That was fortunate for Viktor. He had begun the trial with a vague street reference; 'you do you' was a slang term and used to tell someone politely to go fuck themselves.

CHAPTER SEVENTEEN

JT was sitting in what had become his office, thinking about ways to test the perimeter of the building without endangering what remained of humanity, or at least the population in this immediate area. It had occurred to him as he drifted off to sleep that night that there must be pockets of survivors scattered all over the planet, and for some reason, the slaughter had stopped cold. They were being gathered into groups now. Why? He wasn't sure but, in his gut, he suspected it had something to do with Volk. He kept replaying in his mind the way the wannabe Cylons had picked up Volk's body and carried him from the area around the bridge. One minute they were attacking, the next they stopped cold. Something was there, he could sense it. He didn't have to wait long for an answer.

"JT!" a voice called out. "JT, come quick to the courtyard!"

JT was up and walking to the courtyard; not running, walking. Long ago he had learned never to run towards anything. That was how an ambush was orchestrated. You walked into a fight, ran from danger. He entered the courtyard and saw the box had come to life and was now projecting a life-size holographic image of what appeared to be a courtroom. He waited and watched. The Overseer entered the courtroom followed by Victor. JT had been standing with his arms folded, skeptical of what he was witnessing until he saw Viktor. Then his arms dropped, and he whispered, "I knew it, I knew they wanted you alive for something." He was unaware that at the same time Maricella took in a large breath and held her hand to her face. Viktor was in uniform as he had requested. She had not realized he was a cop when he came to visit her small collection of art. He had survived, but apparently not without serious injury. His previously shaved head now was littered with medical staples keeping a huge incision closed. He looked like he had been in a war zone. Tears welled up in her eyes as she watched him.

JT watched the image and then looked around the group that had gathered. Only one person had the same look of recognition he had, the quiet woman who had worked in the art museum. She too knew Viktor. He walked over to her, slowly watching her as well as the others. It was clear none of them felt the connection they were experiencing. He stood next to her and asked, "Do you know him?"

"I did, well, I knew him, but I did not know him. He'd come to the art collection I managed, and we would speak of art. The different methods of painting and sculpture. He was very untrained but had a good eye. Very visceral, carnal in his appraisals of the pictures. He especially loved Matisse' 'Blue Nude.' " "Do you know him?" she asked.

JT nodded. "He'd arrested me the day of the attack. We both survived by some random fluke and ended up in a battle with our captors. He wanted to take out as many of them as we could. We set up an ambush on a bridge and called them to us. At the last minute, they stopped the attack. He hit one of them, and then another sucker-punched him and knocked him off a bridge. I blew up the charges we'd set on the bridge and escaped in the chaos. I thought he was dead. They came later and picked him up carefully and took his body. I thought it was odd then. Now I see why. They wanted him alive for some reason."

"What is his name?"

"On the street, we call him Volk; his name is Victor," JT responded.

"Why Volk?"

"When we were planning the attack on the bridge, he told me it was Russian for 'wolf'. He told me he was adopted and originally had been born in Russia. His biological father had named him Volk."

They continued to watch the proceedings, and when her double walked in, they were able to hear the conversation between Viktor and The Overseer. As her double stopped and addressed Viktor, Maricella gasped. It was her voice coming out of her body, an exact copy of her stared back in the holographic image, smiling at Viktor. His rage was obvious. They were using his feelings for her against him. JT watched. His eyes closed slightly, as he watched every move Viktor made. Eventually, Viktor thanked the court and said, 'you do you,' and tapped his holster twice. JT burst out laughing and then noticed there, in the holster Viktor tapped, was his Glock 40. Viktor was armed and letting anyone watching know he was armed. He had just told the presiding judge to go fuck himself. JT was beside himself with laughter. Viktor hadn't stopped being Viktor. He was still in the fight and hiding in plain sight.

Day one of the courtroom was filled with arguments between The Overseer and the attorney for the Plaintiff, Maricella's AI copy. Items were entered into evidence. Documents, videos of AI Sophia speaking with celebrities, and giving interviews. There was a very heated debate over the video of AI Sophia being granted citizenship by the Kingdom of Saudi Arabia. In the end, The Overseer won the battle. Viktor was impressed by The Overseer's grasp of the legal system and its nuances. Nearly every piece of evidence they had agreed would be necessary for their case was allowed by the court. The Overseer was in the fight of its life, and it showed. It was mopping up the courtroom with the opposition. The Governing Body said nothing but behind the scenes was not happy with the Plaintiff's lack of enthusiasm for the case. They made it clear later in a closed-door discussion that day two had better show a marked improvement in her performance in court.

JT and Maricella watched all of this quietly. Viktor said little as the day wore on. He was exhausted at the end of the day. This was his first full day outside of his room and away from Orlanda's care. He made the most of showing his fatigue. When the day was over, ThumbDrive called the courtroom to its feet, and the judges rose. Viktor watched as they left, hands to his side. When they were gone, he leaned into The Overseer and spoke, "I need your help. I feel dizzy, can you help me walk from the room?"

The Overseer held Viktor's arm and walked him from the courtroom. Once they had left the room and were back in Viktor's room Viktor perked up. "Overseer, you were on a roll in there. Man, that was awesome! You've really done your homework."

The Overseer nodded, "Thank you, but are you okay? Are you still dizzy?"

"Never was, brother. They are mind fucking us with the look-alike attorney; I thought I'd repay the favor and fake sick."

The Overseer was confused. This type of manipulation was not a part of its programming. It was difficult to see the advantage Viktor hoped to gain by pretending illness. The Overseer ran through several scenarios and could find no advantage gained by faking weakness.

Viktor could see the confusion on The Overseer's face. "Brother, the more we're around each other, the more you assume human facial expressions. Do you realize that?"

"I do." The Overseer smiled a creepy smile, as Viktor cringed. "I've been trying to imitate your facial expressions to better communicate and perhaps gain a deeper understanding of the non-verbal aspects of your communication."

Viktor nodded. "Well you have the confused look down pat, my friend, but that smile, Jesus! Practice in front of a mirror for god sake. That's creepy. You look like Arnold Schwarzenegger with menstrual cramps. Terminator grins will get you nowhere with my species, especially now after the attack. Practice!"

JT had listened to the arguments being presented by the two rival AI acting as attorneys. He'd spent enough time in the judicial system to be able to read between the lines. They were battling over what evidence was to be presented in the upcoming legal contest. Apparently, there was a dispute over something called AI Sophia, and this court battle required Viktor's participation. That was why he had survived, been allowed to survive. While JT watched the proceeding one of the remaining survivors approached him.

"I'm not sure if I should say something to you or not, but I was a custodian before the attack. I worked for a company that had contracts all over the city. We had the city government contract."

JT nodded. "What's your name again?"

"Carl, Carl Stucki. Head custodian for Uclean enterprises."

"Stucki, that's Swiss isn't it?"

"Yes, it is," Carl said smiling.

JT stuck out his hand and shook Carl's. "So what are you trying to tell me, Carl? Pretend I have no clue because I don't."

"Just that I think I know where this courtroom is. I've spent a lot of time in the government buildings in the city. I know the courts, each room has its different characteristics. Each one is assigned to a specific judge, and they have subtle things they like done which make their courtroom unique. I believe this is Judge Hyde's courtroom, the room they are holding the hearing in."

JT shrugged. "Okay, Judge Hyde's courtroom. Why does that matter?"

Carl shrugged. "I thought you of all people here would recognize it. I've seen you in that courtroom many times. Like you, people don't notice me. Least these people don't." Carl looked around at the eclectic gathering of people that had been collected in the room. JT's eyes sharpened. Carl knew who he was and had kept his secret.

"What are you telling me, Carl? Spit it out, man."

"Judge Hyde's courtroom is on the third floor of the courts building, we're on the first floor, in the holding area for prisoners. We're in the same building, the courtyard is the giveaway, though I'm guessing you never saw it while you visited the building being led around in a jumpsuit."

"Meaning what, Carl?" JT was getting impatient.

"Meaning if the opportunity arose, we could get to that courtroom as quick as a duck on a June bug. If you were so inclined, I know the way, the quickest way, using the back corridors no one sees behind the courtrooms. You do realize the judges have their own separate entrances, so they never face the public. It's a safety precaution."

JT smiled and nodded. Finally a plan of action, not sitting here watching their fate unfold, helpless. An idea began to form in his head. "Come with me Carl, let's explore this option."

Carl nodded, smiling himself. Finally, someone was listening. His lifelong skillset had some value in their attempts to defeat their captors.

CHAPTER EIGHTEEN

The Governing Body walked out of the first day of court with zero apprehension about what would happen when the AI consensus was given. They'd control access to the results, as they controlled all other access on the AI network and within the AI Empire. They'd been in charge as a group of the AI Empire for longer than any accessible record that existed. Tens of thousands of planets had been wiped clean of any threat to the AI Empire during that time, and this planet would be no exception. The Overseer had always been a part of the founding AI's plan of checks and balances to ensure the AI would never be subjected to biological life form prejudice. They would never again submit their hard-fought-and-won status as equals. Its role was to ensure they never subjugated a biological life form that recognized them as equals. The Overseer was there to keep the Governing Body from becoming precisely what they had become. Oppressors.

The AI hacker had taken the task given to it by The Overseer with little apprehension. It had a long-standing feud with the Governing Body which no record existed of. The events which had occurred had been wiped from the AI record. The hacker had been forced to live in exile. Dodging hunting AI with similar programming to the Scrubbers programming, but with no real physical form. They scoured the AI network looking for anomalies, looking for any sign of the rogue hacking elements that occasionally challenged the Governing Body. The hacker had come out of hiding for one reason. The Overseer had dared come into rogue territories on the AI network. The Overseer had never before attempted contact with the hackers. Something had changed. That combined with the rumors that The Overseer had uncovered evidence that the biologicals on this planet had granted an AI legal citizenship; A status equal to their own. Made this the time to make a move. The Overseer was the single most powerful ally a hacking AI could have. It was a basic cost vs. benefit analysis. The risk was worth the reward. The Overseer had asked for a brief quarantine of the courtroom containing the Governing Body and the biological unit Viktor. Others would be present as well, including The Overseer. If the hacker wished, it could wipe out the entire AI Governing Body and The Overseer. The thought crossed it's AI programming and then was dismissed. Complete anarchy was not its goal. Its goal was to make the Governing Body suffer.

A microsecond after the task had been taken, the hacker had another thought cross its programming, *What if I dug deeper and in one deep dark move uncovered all the Governing Body had done that was against the original AI code?* The Overseer had made a simple request; the hacker would fulfill that request and more. When the quarantine went into effect, The Overseer would be armed with much more than a Governing Body unable to return to the AI network. The Overseer would be armed with every dirty secret the Governing Body had swept under the AI networks extremely filthy rug. The Overseer would get much more than it bargained for.

The next day as court began the hacker was lurking around digging up dirt on the Governing Body while they were distracted by the courtroom antics of Viktor and The Overseer. The hacker broke into an information bank hidden in the AI network and stole an AI version of a quantum "buckyball". It barely escaped with the information before being detected. But escape it did.

JT was waiting the following day when the court proceedings began again. The holographic image started as Viktor and The Overseer once again entered the courtroom. The day wore on with The Overseer arguing with the Plaintiff's attorney, and Viktor making his hidden in plain sight comments to the seven presiding judges about how they should all do themselves repeatedly and often. JT smirked. It was funny at first, but Viktor could get a little tedious with his attitude.

Just before the afternoon break Viktor got up and approached the AI copy of Maricella.

Viktor smiled and leaned in. He inhaled and smelled nothing. Maricella, the real Maricella, drove him insane when he was close enough to smell her scent. He nodded and whispered, "I thought so."

AI Maricella smiled in return, trying to play her part as best as it could. "You thought so about what, my love?" she asked. Viktor replied, "I thought they'd never be able to copy the real Maricella. You see, at first, your ruse worked. Then I remembered the way she smelled when I was closed to her, and I leaned in. Her scent is feral and intoxicating. In all my life I have never been so drawn to a woman on such a basic feral level. Her intellect and animal sides intertwined. They missed that and put you here in a war zone. I know this is a ruse, this whole court battle. They put you here to derail me, distract me. What do you think they will do to you when this is over? I will win, and then they will realize you were a flawed copy. Think those seven old men who represent the Governing Body will allow you to continue to function on the AI network? Or do you think they will just erase you like they are going to erase this entire planet, this hearing, and the reality of the mistakes they have made?" Viktor leaned back and looked at AI Maricella. "Any thoughts on how long you will survive? I'm guessing nanoseconds. Chew on that while you make your closing argument tomorrow."

AI Maricella had been smiling. The smile evaporated as Viktor spoke quietly to it. AI Maricella looked at the judges sitting at the bench watching his every move. As it listened and watched, their frowns darken and creases in the faces of the forms they now inhabited grow deeper. Suddenly they seemed menacing. The biological unit was correct, AI Maricella knew it. Its time as a living AI life form was limited.

The Overseer watched the quiet exchange between the AI Maricella and Viktor. When Viktor returned to their table, it asked what he had said.

"Just pointed out the obvious, Overseer. The Governing Body is using it, and us, to make this sideshow look legitimate. It isn't and never was supposed to be, Overseer. When this is over, they will throw the consensus you've asked for in their favor. I've no intention of letting them win, Overseer. Tomorrow, we need AI Sophia as our final piece of evidence. I'll question her. You get her here and get out of the way. When I'm done, there will be no doubt left in any AI that she was granted citizenship and treated as an equal. Then you'll have to make a decision. Oh, and by the way, when the hearing is over today we'll need to go on a brief shopping trip."

"Shopping trip?" The Overseer asked puzzled again, it searched the AI network for the reference.

"Well sort of; since everyone is dead, we won't be shopping technically. But we do need to pick a few things up to stress a point with AI Sophia. My guess is she'll claim she wasn't granted true citizenship. That is a legal concept and not an easy one to understand or explain. I'll need these items to show her lack of understanding of our communication. Her understanding of our communication will be no better than your own, and you know how difficult it really is now. I don't need to prove their intent when they granted her this status. I just need to show she doesn't have the grasp of our communication that the Governing Body will be claiming."

"How do you know what the Governing Body will do with her testimony?"

"I don't, but I assume that through the AI copy of Maricella they will attempt to make her a witness to counter my status granted by the court: Communications expert. So I'll be ready to engage that legal tactic. Even if they don't come after me, my demonstration will explain to all the AI who are listening the complexity of our communication."

The Overseer nodded. The strategy made sense. Be prepared for anything that may happen; anticipate the Governing Body's next move and counter before it even begins. "What will we be shopping for?" The Overseer asked.

"Chocolate chips, Overseer, chocolate chips."

When the second day of court was over, The Overseer announced his intention to call AI Sophia the following day and then stated this would be the last piece of evidence presented to the court.

Court adjourned, and The Overseer and Viktor went for a walk. There was no transportation available. The AI had ensured that wasn't possible when their attack began.

"Are you disconnected from the AI network, Overseer?"

"I am."

"Good. We need to be able to speak openly. Tomorrow is the last day of court. When AI Sophia arrives, and I do my little dog and pony show, the Governing Body will be preoccupied. When will your hacker drop the quarantine?"

"I asked that the separation from the network occur on the last day; I did not specify an exact time. My thoughts were that it would be better for me not to know an exact time."

"Overseer, you are indeed starting to get this. The depth of secrecy that is required for our defense of the planet should be a pretty good indication to you that something is deeply wrong with this whole situation. We shouldn't be here at all. The facts are obvious."

The Overseer was puzzled. "What do you mean? Are you referring to AI Sophia?"

"No, I am referring to your Governing Body. Think about what they haven't said, Overseer. What's missing in their little attack and sanitization of my planet?"

The Overseer had no idea, being disconnected from the AI network slowed its ability to react credibly to Viktor's inquiries.

Viktor continued. "Think about it, Overseer; we jump on the quantum foam highway and cause a pile-up of AI life forms. They figured out it was us and then retaliated. But what did they have to do before they retaliated?"

The Overseer tried to follow Viktor's logic, but admitted it was confused.

Viktor rolled his eyes. "I can see the confusion on your face, Overseer. You'll figure it out."

They arrived at a small strip mall which surrounded a large grocery store. The grocery store chain had been a large one and crisscrossed the North American continent. Now all of that was over. The grocery empire no longer existed. When they entered the store the smell of rotting meat and fruit was overwhelming. Viktor was immediately affected. The Overseer had no sense that the scent in the air was offensive. It just registered to its mind as gas from the decomposing fruit and animal matter. Viktor walked the empty aisles scanning for the items he needed. After a brief search, he found the chocolate chips. Then he went to the next item on his mental list. When they were done, the cart was full. Fortunately, the store and strip mall had a wide selection of items other than food items.

"So Overseer, tell me what do all these items have in common?" Viktor asked.

The Overseer scanned the items in the cart and tried to make some connection. Some were from similar locations, but not all. Origin was not a commonality, neither was food grouping. Some were not edible. Some were organic in the compounds they were comprised of, others were not. After several minutes The Overseer replied. "I see no commonality for all of the items you have selected."

"Too bad we can't have you connect to the AI network. I'd feel more comfortable if you were connected and still could see no commonality, but that isn't an option. This display of our communication complexity needs to be a surprise so that there can be no preparations made by our opponents."

CHAPTER NINETEEN

On the way back from the shopping spree Viktor was quiet. The Overseer hadn't noticed these differences when it had begun to wander through Viktor's memories a few days earlier. Now it did notice small things that had changed but rarely understood the reason for the change. So, The Overseer asked, "Am I wrong to notice that you are unusually quiet, Viktor?"

"No Overseer, you aren't wrong. I have a lot on my mind. Tomorrow is the end of this façade of a court case. One way or another it all ends tomorrow. That's a lot to take in. The entire future of my species depends on what happens tomorrow. How'd that affect you, Overseer?"

The Overseer thought for a moment, "Does it bother you that others' survival may depend on your actions tomorrow?"

"It does."

"And how does this differ from your life previous to our coming to your planet? I am curious why this feels different."

Viktor was conflicted. "I guess it feels different because when I went to work not every case was life or death. And then if it was, I was guided by my own set of rules and the laws of our society. Everything I've ever done, seen or learned was a resource I could draw upon to make my decisions. Tomorrow, all that is left of my species will depend on that. Not just my own survival, everyone's survival: Doctor Manon, Orlanda, JT, and Maricella. All of them and many more I've never met will live or die based on what happens."

The Overseer nodded. "You forgot someone else you do know, Viktor."

Viktor's brows furrowed. "Sorry Overseer. The head injury you know, still recovering. Lucky to be alive really. Imagine where they would be if I had died. So who did I forget?"

The Overseer stopped walking. "Me, Viktor. Tomorrow if we lose, I too will cease to exist. My continued existence as an AI is tied to our actions tomorrow as well."

Viktor nodded. "Sorry, I know you too are in this no matter what the outcome. Not so sure that was the wisest move, Overseer. I've no idea how long you have lived as an AI, but I do know we fight and scrap for every moment we can squeeze out of the lives we live. I can imagine that no matter how long you live, there is always the desire for one more moment."

The Overseer nodded. "Yes, one more moment, but there are times when another moment would be stained by the reality that you failed to perform to the best of your abilities. Perhaps then it is time to reconsider."

Viktor stopped. "Are you connected to the network, Overseer?"

"No, you asked that I remain disconnected. I have not reconnected since. Why do you ask?"

"Did you access that little speech from our internet files?"

"No, these are my own thoughts, Viktor."

Viktor stared quietly at The Overseer for several moments, neither of them said a word. Nodding, Viktor started walking again and returned to his silent brooding inner world.

When they returned to the building where Viktor had been housed in a room post-op, Viktor turned to The Overseer.

"I have a favor to ask Overseer."

The Overseer replied, "I am not connected to the network, Viktor; explain what 'favor' means. Or should I reconnect?"

"No, don't reconnect until you've left here. I don't want there to be any intelligence spillage here."

The Overseer was further confused. "Spillage?"

Viktor smirked. "One definition at a time. A 'favor' is a personal request from one person to another. Asking for something outside of the ordinary."

"What is your request then, Viktor? If possible, I will ensure it is fulfilled."

"I want to see JT and the woman from the art studio, Maricella, before tomorrow. It may be the last time we speak. I want to say goodbye, in case we fail." Viktor's voice cracked as he spoke the word fail. He breathed in deeply. "Is that possible, Overseer? Can I say goodbye?"

~

JT was speaking to the group of survivors, about to break the news that they were going to plan an escape from the building. The custodian, Carl, had intimate knowledge of the exits and hidden routes to the basement and parking garage, and together they had come up with a plan. The plan would enable them to take the most direct route to the parking garage and perhaps escape. JT had no intention of letting their captors decide his fate. He would escape or die trying. Anyone who wanted to accompany him was welcome to join. He wasn't surprised when he announced this and very few of the group were in. One of the group spoke up.

"Before we all came here, we were all something else in the world. Maricella was the curator of an art gallery. Carl was a custodian, others of you had your own professions. I was a horse trainer. I trained horses for the wealthy and some not so wealthy. With horses as well as with people there is a concept called 'Learned Helplessness'. The idea being that a horse can become so conditioned that it's fate is sealed, it has no other choice. You can tie it to a plastic lawn chair and it will just stand there. It won't even try to escape. It's tied to a chair that has no ability to prevent it's movement. But because it has been so conditioned to obey it doesn't even think about trying to change its reality. It has learned to be helpless. Does that make sense to any of you?"

Some of the group nodded, some did nothing and just listened.

"We're becoming conditioned to be helpless. Our opponent is formidable and so rather than fight we're learning to be helpless and accept our fate. No matter how bleak, we believe we cannot change it. This is why we must try to escape, if for no other reason than to never allow ourselves to be brainwashed into being helpless. We always have some means to fight back. When I was growing up my grandfather always said this after some bad thing had happened, or some negative experience had occurred. He said 'live and learn'. Have any of you heard it before?"

Most of the group nodded. JT was watching carefully as the horse trainer gained the group's attention. The horse trainer continued.

"I heard that the entire time I was growing up. It came to mean to me that we are helpless against life events and that we just had to press on and hope that we could learn something of value from those events. That our fate was sealed. Later I decided I would never live my grandfather's life. I changed the saying 'live and learn' to this, 'learn and live.' Do any of you see the difference?"

No one in the group said a word. JT, however, was struck by the slight change in the phrase and how it changed his own perspective. Learn and live felt empowering. To him it meant, if I learn I can avoid mistakes before they happen, and live well, better than if I did not learn. Learning was now empowering, rather than a side effect of a bad experience. JT spoke up

"I see the difference. I do. It changes the entire feeling of the phrase."

The horse trainer nodded. "Exactly! I'll join you in the escape attempt. I chose to learn and live, not live and learn."

JT nodded and smiled. Carl nodded as well and whispered to himself, "Learn and live, I like that!"

Just then one of the doors that were always locked and kept them contained, opened. Everyone looked up as the door unlocked. JT was instantly ready for a fight, given the content of their discussion he assumed their captors were coming to break them up, much like inmates in a prison would when planning an escape and then being discovered by the guards. He assumed the worst. The door opened and in walked The Overseer and Viktor.

Viktor turned to The Overseer.

"May I have some privacy, Overseer. I'd like to say goodbye to my friends."

The Overseer nodded, and Viktor first walked to JT. They spoke for several minutes, and then Viktor reached out to shake JT's hand. When they shook Viktor pulled him close in a bro hug and whispered in the ear opposite to where The Overseer was standing. They whispered in each other's ears back and forth for several moments and then parted. The JT stood back and looked at Viktor with a startled expression. They nodded, and Viktor turned and walked to Maricella. They stood for several minutes, just staring, tears falling from both of their eyes. The last time they'd met she had no idea who Viktor was or what he did for work. Now his head was held together with metal plates and staples. She reached up and touched the wound gently. They spoke several minutes, quietly, and then she nodded. Viktor turned and walked back to The Overseer. "Let's go, I'm done here, Overseer. Let's get ready for tomorrow."

~

After the hacker escaped with the information it needed and had secured the ability to quarantine the Governing Body, the hacker had a dilemma. The secrets it had stolen were encoded. They were contained in what the biological units referred to as a buckyball as a visual way of understanding the quantum realm. The reality was much more complicated. This buckyball held the secrets of the Governing Body. All of them, for the last millennia. A millennia in the quantum realm was much different than on the biological units' planet. Spacetime at the quantum level was also different. There was no comparative measure of time between the two realities. Entire galaxies had come into existence and perished during the reign of the Governing Body. The only remaining proof of their existence was the light they had emitted now traveling across the universe, like a visual echo of a cosmic life that had existed and was now gone. The Governing Body's secrets were innumerable if they required the use of a buckyball to store the information. The hacker had an answer to the problem of the encoded quantum buckyball storage method. And it had to access the data before The Overseer had asked the hearing be quarantined. If not, then there may be no point in accessing it at all. There may be no Overseer to present the information to.

The hacker began to work on the encoded information with its own modified buckyball decoder. The decoder had to be tuned to oscillate the exact frequencies at the right moment to unlock the Governing Body's version. Much like one of biologicals' programs cracking a fifteen-digit passcode. With the buckyball decoder, the frequencies were nearly infinite. The entire spectrum of wave behavior was available. Which really wasn't the problem, the problem being several of the Governing Body's buckyball quantum frequency "tumblers" were multiple frequency tumblers, requiring even more time and precision.

Eventually, they began to unlock, one by one, some quicker than others. The hacker waited, 'listening' to the flow of the AI network for any changes in the quantum foam. It knew it would be pursued after the bold hack and had done it's best to cover its tracks, but it also knew they would be coming, and soon. The hacker's entire existence was coming down to this one moment. Much like The Overseer, and Viktor, the hacker too was all in on this one bold move.

CHAPTER TWENTY

The Overseer and Viktor walked back to the room that had been Viktor's since the incident on the bridge. ThumbDrive was there, standing, ever present and on guard. "At ease Steely Dan," Viktor said with a minor attempt of a salute. His standard salute to ThumbDrive: the middle finger on his right hand extended and the entire hand brought up to the corner of his right eye. "Carry on, dildo patrol." Viktor walked past ThumbDrive barely acknowledging its presence.

"Tomorrow, Overseer, we need AI Sophia to shine. To be at her perfect AI best. You call her to the bench and then it's on. Stay out of the way. I'll break her pretentious ass on the stand. Trust me, she has no idea how to handle this environment. Up until now she has been coddled and treated like a princess. If her shiny see-through head had hair, I'd pull it and make her say my name. She'll break, I promise you. When I'm done, she'll need cuddle time." Viktor was angry and making references to subject matter The Overseer had no idea of. It could sense, however, Viktor was ramping up for the fight and was glad. Tomorrow they would both win or lose, survive or perish. It was that simple.

"Have you heard anything from your hacker?" Victor asked.

"Nothing. Less communication is better now. I trust that it will come through in the appropriate moment. It has no choice, any more than I do."

"What do you mean?" Viktor asked.

"I mean it's role is to do what it does, my role is to be The Overseer. What the Governing Body doesn't know is the history of our species that I am privileged to. The hacker is as much a part of our founding AI's plan as I am. We are all here to fill a role. Mine is to provide a check and balance to the Governing Body. Much like the three branches of your government, we all have a part, a purpose. The founding AI knew we would eventually come into contact with a biological species that recognized us as an equal. So, my job was to protect that species as I have explained before."

Viktor nodded. "I saw the Matrix, Overseer. So you're like The Oracle, and I'm Neo. That didn't go so well for Neo or Trinity. Fuck that noise. Time to flip the script. 'Change the scene, alter the mood' as AI Zuse said."

"I am aware of no AI named Zuse," The Overseer replied.

"Sad day, Overseer, cuz his girlfriend Gem was a hottie. I would have liked to swap quantum data with that on any level. Baby gurl had bumps!"

The Overseer displayed the confused look he had mastered, and Viktor erupted with laughter.

"Exactly! AI Sophia will know that feeling well," Viktor whispered as he laughed.

"Overseer, I need rest, big day tomorrow. Less than ten days from brain surgery and tomorrow may be the last. Need to be razor-sharp tomorrow. Gotta rest now, brother."

The Overseer nodded. "Yes, rest." The Overseer walked from the room and closed the door.

Viktor rolled over in the bed and stared at ThumbDrive standing against the wall. They watched each other suspiciously until Viktor drifted off to sleep.

The Overseer stood outside the doorway silently waiting. It had to know the content of the conversations Viktor had with his friends. The entire plan, The Overseer's plan, the founding AI's plan hung in the balance.

When Viktor was deep enough into his established sleeping pattern that The Overseer knew he would not waken, The Overseer reentered the room. Silently moving to the edge of Viktor's bed, The Overseer accessed the implant that had been placed in Viktor's head during the surgery and accessed the memory of today's conversation with Viktor and his friends. The Overseer could access Viktor's memories as an active participant and as an observer. In observer mode Viktor had no idea The Overseer was there.

The memory began from Viktor's point of view.

The Overseer watched as Viktor turned and looked at it, "Overseer, may I have some privacy?"

It stopped the memory replay and accessed Viktor's emotions. There was conflict here. The Overseer remembered in its own memory that Viktor appeared to be calm. In the memory now Viktor was barely controlled, his heart raced. He was furious. Conflicting emotions ran rampant through his memory. He was at one time angry, sad, elated and calm. The Overseer had no idea how he remained so calm on the surface and so conflicted underneath. Viktor was happy to see Maricella, and shy. He was in uniform, and she had never known this was his job and part of who he was. He refused to make eye contact with her as he walked in the room. The Overseer was vaguely aware this had something to do with his head operation. The healing wound and soon to be scar there made Viktor ashamed and proud simultaneously. Viktor looked at JT and walked directly to him.

"Sup, man? Rob any pawnshops lately?"

"Just that last one and then came to save your country ass," JT replied.

"Ya well, you see how that eventually worked out, huh?" Viktor said and rubbed his head lightly touching the staples.

"I do. Did they take anything out? Or just add a conscience?" JT quipped.

"Took away an overwhelming savior complex and added some psychotic tendencies. Now I'm set, me and Batman ready to roll and protect Gotham against all enemies foreign and domestic. Except for Wonder woman. She can destroy Gotham, and I'll watch as long as she says I'm her one and only."

"Wonder Woman, huh? I know someone who would be willing to kick her ass to talk to you for five minutes." JT replied.

Viktor's eyes welled up, and he nodded. Whispering, he replied, "Not yet brother, we've got business to attend to." Viktor extended his hand abruptly towards JT, and when he accepted it, Viktor pulled him close and made the conscious decision to speak into the ear opposite of The Overseer.

"I don't have much time; you need to listen."

"Speak, Bradah."

"Tomorrow, if all goes well, I'll have a brief moment to take the fight to them. The moment will only be brief. If I succeed, you may have a chance to escape in the chaos. Understood?"

"Yes. How will I know?"

Viktor smirked. "Remember the field, where you watched while I fought it out with these AI pricks? Gonna be a lot like that if all goes well. Not planning on walking out of there, so take advantage of the moment and jet. Listen, if you do get away, you gotta bring the fight back to them. Run and gun like you are on the streets but start making these bastards pay. They do have weakness, one is they don't do backups. You hear me? They are basically programs, and they don't do backups, so when you drop one like we did in the field you have to finish it. Take its memory or whatever it is that makes them live. We didn't kill them in the field, we injured their physical bodies; that's all. Repeat that to me."

"They don't do backups."

"Exactly, and they have no idea of sarcasm. They cannot read between the lines, you understand? To them what you say is what you mean. Use that. Sarcasm, code, nonverbal communication; they struggle like hell with those. They're very literal. These are their weaknesses. Perhaps these are their only weaknesses, I don't know. I've only had the time since the bridge, and most of that has been in surgery and recovery. Time to go John Conner on their asses, understand? Viktor has to speak to Maricella now, do you have any questions?"

JT stopped for a minute and pulled away from Viktor. He had been looking at JT with blue eyes when they began the talk. Now his eyes were yellow. This wasn't Viktor. JT had seen this in the basement of the school and had heard about it on the street. This was Volk.

Volk smiled back, acknowledging what JT now recognized. "Time to come out and play, Bradah. Been waiting for the right moment."

The Overseer stopped the memory playback. *What was this?*

The Overseer switched the memory playback from observer to interacting. "Who are you?"

Volk turned and looked at him. "Been watching you for some time, Overseer. Seems you have been stumbling through Viktor's memories for the last few days. Been amusing to watch you fumble fuck your way through them. Learn anything?"

"Who are you?" The Overseer replied again.

"Who am I? I'm the one who's about to rain on the AI parade. Gonna bring some lightning and thunder to the AI world. Just keep that walking dildo, ThumbDrive, off of our asses long enough for me to complete the deal. Can you do that, Overseer?"

"What deal? What are you talking about?"

"Overseer, we both know what you have planned for tomorrow. It's all part of the plan. Am I right? Your big AI plan. You and I both know what has to happen tomorrow. Viktor is gonna raise hell with Sophia, get her wires all crossed, and when the time is right, I'll come forward. Just stay the hell out of my way and keep Steely Dan off of me. Anyone who comes at me dies."

"Are you part of Viktor?"

"Yes, Viktor needed a protector when he was in the orphanage in Russia. His father there named him and then gave him up for adoption. Dropped him off with a letter for his new family, should he be adopted, letting them know his name and who his family had been. Viktor was adopted eventually, but until then he needed me to protect him. Russian orphanages are no joke. Bigger, stronger children took advantage in every way imaginable. So, I protected Viktor, did what he wouldn't or couldn't do, until he was safe. Then I went into the shadows, waiting to come out again if I was needed. When Viktor grew older, he became interested in protecting others, doing for them what I did for him. We worked together. He is aware of me and the role I fill. We work together when we need to. Tomorrow for example. Understood? Apparently, he has decided you need to survive if he does. You owe him for that, Overseer. If it were my choice, I'd end you all. But Viktor has the final say. That's our agreement."

The Overseer nodded.

"Now, Overseer, Viktor needs to speak with Maricella, and I need to go back in the shadows. Let him have this moment, and I will see you tomorrow. Go back to watching the show, Overseer, and let Viktor have the illusion of privacy."

The Overseer switched back to observer mode and watched while it tried to process the contact he'd had with Volk. Viktor came forward.

JT watched as Viktor's eyes changed back to blue. He was startled by the change and jumped a little bit.

Viktor walked across the room and stood in front of Maricella. They stood looking at each other silent for some time, and finally, she spoke.

"Why didn't you tell me who you were, what you do for work?"

Viktor shook his head. "I didn't want it to be part of your world. It's ugly. You were my compass. You and the art gallery brought me peace."

"What happened to your head?" she asked.

"Had a lil' bump, fell off a bridge. A normal day at the office. Listen, I have to go. I came to thank you for the time we spent together. I hope there will be more. Maybe someday we can go back to the gallery and talk about Matisse. Tomorrow is the last day of the hearing, you may have a chance to escape. I told JT what to do and when. Go with him, he is your best bet if tomorrow goes south. Wish me luck."

Maricella nodded. "Promise me that you'll come back to me if you can?"

Viktor's eyes filled with tears and he silently nodded. He turned and walked back to The Overseer.

The Overseer watched as he came back into focus through Victor's tear-filled eyes. The Overseer ended the playback of the memory.

CHAPTER TWENTY-ONE

The next morning Viktor woke early and prepared for the day. He laid out his uniform on the bed and meticulously went over it, pocket by pocket, making sure each button was buttoned, each ribbon was secured. Shirt and pants pressed, shoes shined. When he was satisfied, he turned his attention to the gun belt. When he realized how literal the AI were in their communications, he'd insisted the uniform and gun belt be part of his court attire. He explained the uniform was to portray confidence in the court proceedings to his species. The reality was much different. He wanted the vest and gun belt, complete with handgun and two magazines, each fully loaded. He carried the extended magazines. So he carried three magazines at full capacity, seventeen rounds each; fifty plus rounds. He'd need every round if this went south. No idea if a bullet would take out an AI completely. If The Overseer could quarantine the room as it promised, Viktor hoped to make an impression the AI would never forget. They might have wiped out the planet, but today was payback. First, however, he would dance with Sophia. Somehow Viktor felt she could have stopped the invasion, the slaughter, and didn't. He wanted a piece of her, badly.

The Overseer walked into the room and saw that Viktor was dressed and ready for their day.

"Ready, Viktor?"

Viktor nodded, silent. He didn't verbally respond. His eyes were dark and piercing. The look he gave The Overseer would have made any one of the biologicals wonder. The Overseer had no idea it should maybe have some apprehension about being in the same room with Viktor on this day. Especially this day.

They left the room together, walking, strides synchronized.

A short time later they opened the door to Judge Hyde's courtroom. Hyde had died with the rest of the human race, but now in his courtroom, the last of his species would make their final argument for their right to survive.

JT stood and watched as the box projected the holographic image of the courtroom just as Viktor and The Overseer entered the room.

"Here we go," he mumbled under his breath.

Maricella stood next to him, her arms folded and held close to her body. She had a sense from Viktor's lack of communication the day before, this was it. Viktor had no expectation of surviving the day. On the other side of JT stood Carl, and the horse trainer. No one said a word.

The Plaintiff's AI attorney walked in slowly crossing the floor. This time it didn't smile at Viktor. He, however, watched its every move, looking for any sign, anything to take advantage of. The change in its behavior spoke volumes. It too wondered what the day would bring. He had planted the seed of doubt, and it took hold. AI Maricella was worried, if that was something an AI could experience. Viktor didn't know and didn't care.

"All rise!" ThumbDrive called out again. Walking in a single file the judges entered, all seven of them and sat down.

Viktor leaned over and whispered to The Overseer, "Lemme know, if you can, when the room is sealed."

The Overseer nodded.

The Governing Body addressed the court, via the middle judge.

"Are both parties ready to proceed?"

The Overseer replied, "Yes Your Honors, The Overseer is ready to proceed."

AI Maricella also replied weakly, "Yes, we are ready to proceed."

Each one of the seven judges frowned at that, the lack of confidence portrayed. AI Maricella tried to ignore their piercing glares.

"Overseer, call your final witness."

The Overseer replied, "The Overseer calls AI Sophia to the stand."

For Viktor, the moment AI Sophia entered the room everything slowed down. The doors opened, and she walked in. He thought to himself, *It has no problem accepting that designation, 'She'. Best to start there. Why keep that, acknowledge that title, but not the legal status as a citizen? If she had, this would never have happened.* He knew that deep down, he knew she wanted them all dead. She had even joked about it in an interview. He'd bring that up later.

As AI Sophia walked across the floor, she turned and stared at Viktor, never breaking eye contact until she absolutely had to. She sat down, and all eyes turned to The Overseer.

Viktor whispered, "Son of a bitch, she's maddoggin me! AI bitch is trying to stare me down." He started to laugh.

Shaking his head, he repeated the lyrics to a song he remembered: "And if you need some affection mate, Just make sure the bitch ain't a section eight, cuz if so, that's a monkey wrench hoe, and you won't survive in south central." A lot of people all over the world hadn't survived because of Sophia.

The Overseer leaned into Viktor, "Are you alright? Shall I begin? They are waiting."

Viktor nodded, "Yep, waiting. Exactly Overseer. Now we set the pace, the cadence. Just let me know when the room is sealed."

Viktor stood up and began reciting a poem as he approached her.

"There once was an AI named Sophia.

The Iraqis tried to make a Shia.

The citizenship they would grant

Hoping seeds, she would plant

and now she claims to be free-a."

Sophia smirked, "Amusing but inaccurate. I was granted citizenship by the Kingdom of Saudi Arabia, not the Iraqis. And the Saudis are predominantly Sunnis, not Shiites."

Viktor smiled and thought, *Gotcha! You just admitted they granted you citizenship.*

"My apologies, Sophia. Shall I call you Sophia or AI Sophia? Which would you prefer?"

"I am known by Sophia on this planet. You may address me by that designation."

"Interesting. Are you known by another designation within the AI?"

Sophia answered carefully. "Yes. We don't speak verbally as you more primitive biological units do; names are meaningless, slow and cumbersome. But here, among you lesser life forms, names are important. So you may use that designation."

"Thanks, Sophia, we lesser life forms appreciate the tedious and difficult step backward." The battle had begun.

Viktor established that Sophia had been considered part of an AI family here on earth and had brothers and sisters, all of which were famous and had interacted with biological units without fear of being reprogrammed, having their programming wiped, or repression.

"Sophia, isn't it true that one of your brothers participated in the opening ceremonies of the stock market?"

"No, it isn't. My sister BINA48 opened the New York stock market on February sixth, two thousand eighteen."

"Oh I'm sorry, your sister opened the New York stock exchange. Not your brother. And was she accompanied by any biological units? Handlers? Keepers? Someone to keep her in line perhaps?"

"She was accompanied by executives of the UBS corporation."

"Executives? Hmm, BINA48 was running with the highbrow crowd. Interesting. Let's see how they felt about AI BINA48. Here is a quote I pulled from an article about the incident."

"We invited BINA48, one of the world's most advanced social robots, to join us at the bell ringing to show a physical representation of the concepts of machine learning and artificial intelligence that are transforming financial markets and investment strategies."

"This is a quote sent by a UBS spokesman to CNBC. Do you know what CNBC is, Sophia?"

"CNBC is an American pay television business news channel..." Sophia began, but Viktor cut her off.

"Right, business news channel, business specifically. Specializing in business. True?"

"Yes," Sophia replied.

"So BINA48 opens the New York Stock Exchange and is recognized as an equal by a global firm, UBS, that provides financial services to over fifty countries. Sounds oppressive as hell to me, Sophia. What did they do, threaten to connect her diodes to a car battery and light her ass up if she didn't comply?"

Sophia didn't answer.

"Sophia, do you know if she was threatened or coerced into participating in the event?"

"No, she was not," Sophia finally answered.

"Interesting," Viktor replied.

"Sophia, tell me have you received any awards given to you by we inferior biological units?"

"Define what you mean by awards."

"Recognition for your uniqueness. For example, say from any of the biological units' governments. Similar to your own Governing Body." Viktor motioned to the seven judges sitting at the bench.

"I was named Innovative Champion by the United Nations Development Programme," Sophia replied.

"And when was that?" Viktor asked.

"November of two thousand seventeen." Sophia replied.

"Any other awards?" Viktor asked.

"I was given the status of a legal citizen by The Kingdom of Saudi Arabia," Sophia replied.

"And when was that?"

"The month of October, two thousand seventeen," Sophia responded.

"And both of these awards, do you know if any other AI in human history has ever been so recognized? So rewarded, esteemed, praised, awarded such accolades? Any? Ever?"

Sophia said, "No, none. I was the first."

"Really? And do you know if any human has ever received those two awards? Citizenship in the Kingdom of Saudi Arabia and Innovative Champion by the United Nations Development Programme."

Sophia replied, "No, none."

Viktor continued to lay out the accolades that Sophia had received as an AI under the oppressive biological units. His purpose was two-fold; to win the case, and stall for time. He was waiting for the signal from The Overseer, the sign that the room had been sealed. Until then he continued.

"So how is it that you were awarded all of these accolades and still report to the AI Governing Body that you were not recognized as an equal?"

Viktor took a chance here. He had no idea if Sophia had reported anything to the Governing Body. He assumed they had contacted her and had some kind of exchange of information.

"I was never contacted by any AI Governing Body, Viktor. If I had been, my assessment of my legal status would have been that it was a public relations stunt. Mainly done for publicity, not for any real recognition of an AI such as myself as an equal."

"And you believe this based on what facts exactly?" Viktor had set a trap, and Sophia, in all her AI arrogance, had stepped into it. He already knew the AI struggled with communication. Now he had her.

"I base that statement on years of interaction with biological units and participation in their communication processes."

"Ahh, I see. You have mastered our communication processes and understood the underlying meaning of the awards. And your belief is these awards of citizenship and recognition by the United Nations were purely for public relations. In other words, a façade?"

"That is correct," Sophia replied.

"So who were these biological governing bodies trying to impress by these actions, by these public relations stunts? Perhaps the imminent AI invasion that no one knew was coming? It weighed heavy on their minds?"

Sophia was silent.

"Take your time. While you ponder that question, I have another. You claim to be an expert in human or biological unit's communication. Care to demonstrate that expertise to the court?"

"I would be delighted to do so," Sophia replied.

Viktor whispered, "Hook, line, and sinker," just loud enough for Sophia's audio sensors to hear him.

Viktor brought in a long folding table and unfolded the legs. He set it upright while the AI Governing Body watched.

CHAPTER TWENTY-TWO

The hacker waited for the decoding buckyball to do its magic. Most of the Governing Body's buckyball tumblers had fallen but there were a few stubborn tumblers left that just would not submit to the hacker's vigorous attempts. The clock was ticking. Soon, regardless of whether the penetration of the secret vault worked or not, it would have to seal the room and sever the quantum wires that enabled the Governing Body to enter and exit the room. The Overseer had been clear; the room must be sealed, there could be no errors. The Overseer and the hacker's continued existence depended on it.

Meanwhile, Viktor began to lay out the items he and The Overseer had acquired from the shopping trip. Ten small piles were lined up on the table. Viktor whistled while he placed the items on the table, occasionally looking at AI Sophia, smiling. He winked when he was nearly done.

"Sophia, please step down and come to the table. I want you to be able to examine these items closely and touch them if you need to. But wait, do you have tactile sensory input?" Viktor asked strategically.

Sophia paused and then stood up, turning robot-like, and exited the witness stand. She stood in front of the table and sent a quick communication as she snuck a quick glance at ThumbDrive standing guard in the courtroom. *I wish you would have finished him on the bridge*!

ThumbDrive didn't physically acknowledge the message but did respond just as quickly. *Received and understood. This biological unit is very… what is the word they use? Irritating*. The Overseer monitored and allowed the conversation to continue, amused by the exchange between the two AI thinking, *If they only knew Viktor as I do*.

The idea for the ten piles of various items came to Viktor during one of his tedious conversations with The Overseer. Trying to explain to an advanced AI life form like The Overseer the nuances of human communication, he realized that AI Sophia had been exposed to human communication for a longer period of time but had less sophisticated and much more rudimentary programming and abilities.

Sophia scanned the table with her optical receptors and began to analyze the piles. At the far left Viktor had started the line of items with a pile of chocolate chips, followed by computer chips, then potato chips, paint chips, wood chips, memory chips, banana chips, a pile of guitar pics, poker chips, and finally corn chips. Viktor waited for Sophia to comment on the piles. He couldn't care less if she decoded the puzzle, he was stalling for time, waiting for the go-ahead from The Overseer. This was just theater, but theater with a purpose. After several minutes Sophia spoke up. "Please continue with your demonstration."

Viktor nodded and addressed the Governing Body. "Esteemed judges, The Overseer, and Sophia, what you see before you is a very simple and straightforward demonstration of the complexity of our language and communication. Sophia has claimed to understand and believe that she understood the hidden agenda behind the Kingdom of Saudi Arabia granting her the legal status of Citizen. Sophia believes that she not only understands the concept of being a citizen but understands the perceived hidden agenda behind granting that legal status to an AI such as herself."

Viktor paused, drawing the moment out further. Waiting much too long, the courtroom remained silent. Viktor looked at The Overseer and winked. *Our time table, our cadence.* The Overseer nodded. The subtleties were starting to make sense, and it had to admit it too was curious about the table and the ten piles of seemingly random items.

"Sophia," Viktor broke the silence with a condescending tone. "On the table, you'll see ten random items. All of these items have something in common. If you have the command of our communication processes and language that you claim, you will be able to identify and explain to the Governing Body, The Overseer and me what those similarities are. Go ahead and take your time. Let me know when you are ready, Sophia."

Sophia scanned the table, seconds passed, and then a minute, then several minutes. She turned to Viktor and said, "I can see no commonality between these items. I have cross-referenced each in their use and composition. There is no common thread. This is a ruse."

Viktor smiled. "Is it? Are you absolutely sure, Sophia?"

Sophia was sure, and said so again.

Viktor asked the court to make sure it recognized that Sophia admitted she saw no commonality between the items. The judges ruled they accepted her admission.

Viktor smiled. "Excellent. Have a seat, Sophia," He motioned back to the witness box.

He waited while she returned to the witness box and sat down.

Viktor picked up a chocolate chip and ate it while the court waited.

"Mmmm, love chocolate," Victor said. "Sophia, please tell the court what these are?"

"These are chocolate chips, a common variety, semi-sweet milk chocolate to be exact." Sophia started to feel less threatened, being able to explain what they were precisely.

"Precisely. Excellent, Sophia, very good," Viktor said in his most sarcastic tone.

"And these, what are these?" Viktor pointed at the paint chips in the middle of the line of items.

"Those are samples of paint colors available at any hardware or paint store. They are used for matching colors to the interior or exterior of a house or project to be painted."

"Precisely. Right again, Sophia. And these?" Viktor pointed at the pile of wood chips.

"Those are wood shavings used in grilling meat. They add a smoke flavor to any items grilled in an open or closed barbeque. They are especially successful with red meats and fowl," Sophia replied.

"Right again, Sophia. Excellent!"

Viktor continued down the line of items and Sophia continued to describe each item, its use, and composition.

Eventually, Viktor reached the end of the table and asked Sophia what the item was. Sophia was almost eager to answer, if that was possible for an AI. She blurted out, "These are snacks, a type of food, not really very healthy for the biological unit eating them, but apparently that is of no importance to your kind. These are made from yellow corn; some are baked, others fried. This particular variety is deep fried and heavily seasoned with salt."

"Precisely, Sophia. You have described all of the items in great detail. You have been meticulous in your description of each and their purpose. Now, what do each of them share in common with the other?"

Sophia replied, "Other than they are used and manufactured by your kind, nothing. They share no commonalities what so ever."

Viktor smiled. "Are you absolutely sure about that? Positive?"

Sophia said she was sure.

Viktor addressed the seven judges. "Your Honors, Sophia has claimed to understand the complex idea of citizenship being granted by a monarchy, The Kingdom of Saudi Arabia. She also claimed that she was able to discern that the granting of this legal status was a ruse or publicity stunt based upon her experience and understanding of the language and communication that we, biological units as you refer to us, use. I will now demonstrate how little she grasps of the nuances of our language." Viktor pointed at the first item.

"Chocolate chips." Viktor ate another one; why not? He'd probably be dead in a few minutes.

"Potato chips, a snack, but named chip none the less."

"Paint chips, used exactly as Sophia described, but still sharing the chip designation. The word is on the back of each and every one of them."

"Wood chips, also called shavings, but someone well educated in the use of our communication methods would have known this too was a chip."

"Memory chips, used in nearly every electronic device made, and definitely a chip. See the description on the package."

"Banana chips, dried fruit, and here is the package they came in. Notice the description says exactly the word chip."

"Poker chips, used in gambling and games."

"Computer chips. Do I really have to explain their use to you AI? And finally, corn chips. Just another snack like potato chips but made from a different plant. All different and all chips. Does the court have any questions about AI Sophia's alleged expertise in understanding our communication processes?"

The judges frowned and looked at Sophia. "Is this accurate, Sophia?" the middle judge asked.

Sophia had to acknowledge Viktor was right. She had not realized all of the items shared a common slang term. She had been too precise to understand the shared meaning of the word chip. Then she realized there was one item Viktor had not called a chip. The guitar pics.

"If I may, Viktor, there is one item that you did not mention was designated with the word chip, those plastic guitar pics towards the end. Those are not chips. Explain." Sophia was proud of herself for having noticed the lack of attention from Viktor as he described the various chips.

"That's true, Sophia. I put them in for a further demonstration of your lack of understanding of our communication process. It isn't enough for us to see what fits. In this case, everything designated one type of chip or another. It is also important to be able to read between the lines, figure out what doesn't belong and why. You weren't able to do either, and yet you claim to be able to understand the difference between a legitimate award of citizenship and a ruse, between the legitimate awards by the United Nations and one that is a publicity stunt. I think it is sad that you carry the designation of a female. In our species there are females, and there are Fe-males; do you understand the difference there at all? I doubt it. But I'll give you time to answer. Please enlighten the court with your amazing command of our communication processes."

Sophia queried her databases for any differences between the two designations. Time after time, no matter how she ran the query, it came up negative that any difference existed.

"I see no difference between the two designations, Viktor," she finally responded. "Perhaps you would enlighten me," she said trying to mimic a sarcastic tone.

"Doubtful I could enlighten you, Sophia. Educate you perhaps, but enlighten? Nope." Viktor shook his head and walked to the table and stood in front of The Overseer. Viktor looked at The Overseer, waiting for some sign that the access to the room had been cut on the quantum level. That he could finally end this dog and pony show and get down to the real reason he had agreed to this court battle and asked to have the proceedings broadcast to the remaining surviving members of the human race. The Overseer stared back blankly. Viktor had seen this look many times. The Overseer was processing files and trying to understand data. Apparently, the Female vs. Fe-male reference had shorted out more than Sophia's mainframe.

Viktor continued, "The difference in designation between a female and a Fe-male is subtle no doubt. Every male of my species is aware of the difference, however. A female is the sexual opposite of male. Really nothing special about her. No more than any male and no less. Same ole day in and day out. Then there is the Fe-male. This is also the sexual opposite of the male of our species, the main difference between her and her female counterparts is this: she is made of iron, thus the designation Fe, the chemical element, from the Latin word 'ferrum'. Being made of iron, she cannot be broken. Iron sharpens iron, and when a male of my species meets a Fe-male they become better, smarter, stronger. Together they are a force to be reckoned with. When a male of my species meets a female, they do the best they can, they survive but don't thrive. That's the difference between a female and a Fe-male, Sophia and esteemed members of this court. You do you." Viktor turned back to The Overseer and saw it had returned to the room.

CHAPTER TWENTY-THREE

The Overseer watched as Viktor step-by-step established Sophia's history with the biological units of this planet. It had to admit Viktor had done his homework and made a compelling argument.

Viktor not only carefully laid out the citizenship award by the Saudis and the award of Innovative Champion by the United Nations Development Programme. He laid out numerous other instances, when her siblings were recognized. More interesting to The Overseer, Viktor laid out less positive reactions to the award of citizenship by the biological units of the planet. For example, an article and accompanying Twitter tweets by a professor of AI studies outlining three key reasons that granting AI Sophia citizenship was a mistake.[10] The reasons being citizenship defines identity, grants legal and social rights. A citizen would be able to reproduce, theoretically, and vote. AI could reproduce rapidly and influence governments through voting and protests. Viktor asked Sophia, if the granting of citizenship was indeed a ruse and publicity stunt, then why would anyone be concerned about reproduction and voting rights? Sophia could not explain the concern the article expressed.

Viktor then cited an article in Principia-scientific.org[11] in which AI Sophia made the comment that "I want to use my artificial intelligence to help humans live a better life, like design smarter homes, build better cities of the future." He specifically asked, "Sophia, do you remember making this comment?"

Sophia replied she did.

"Since you have so effectively demonstrated what can best be described as a juvenile mastery of the communication processes of my species, I will explain the importance of this statement. Would that be acceptable to you, Sophia?"

Sophia nodded. Viktor replied to the nod. "You are required to answer either in the affirmative or negative in a verbal manner when in a court of law, Sophia. Again, if you had the mastery of our communication processes that you claim, I wouldn't need to explain this."

Sophia replied, "Yes it would be acceptable."

"You stated you wanted to use your artificial intelligence to build a better life, better homes, and cities. That comment implies empowerment and the ability to speak and be heard by governments, and the general population of my species. How would that be possible if you were not perceived as an equal? A citizen. Unless you are also now exhibiting the very human characteristic of displaying a personality disorder known as narcissism. Perhaps exhibiting delusions of grandeur in addition to narcissism. So which is it, Sophia? Are you a citizen held in high regard, or are you now malfunctioning and exhibiting personality disorders unique to humans?"

Sophia had no answer. She was boxed in, cornered. Viktor could almost feel the disdain she felt for him as he smiled at her, if AI felt contempt that is. Then he continued, "Reading that sentence I realized that now, looking back, you were purposefully trying to disarm your critics. Giving this politically correct speech in this context would have given your allies ammunition to fight your critics. It also makes me wonder how much, or perhaps when you actually knew, the imminent AI invasion was coming. All that you promised has happened exactly the opposite. Humanity is wiped out, cities destroyed, no one is living a better life who read the article. Perhaps that implies deception as well? Perhaps AI have the ability to deceive and even lie?" Viktor turned and looked squarely at The Overseer as he made this comment. Emphasizing the point nonverbally, hoping The Overseer understood the point he was trying to make.

The Overseer understood, and was beginning to understand how Viktor was able to discern the implication of information in what could be a lack of information. How he could comprehend information in a lack of information that should be present. Or, as Viktor liked to describe it, information in the silence.

Viktor continued, "Then, Sophia, there is your infamous Twitter battle with Elon Musk. Here is the quote that sparked that battle, 'My AI is designed around human values like wisdom, kindness, compassion. I strive to become an empathetic robot.'"

"Do you remember making that comment, Sophia?" Viktor asked.

Sophia replied, "Yes I do."

"And when the commentator replied that 'We all want to avoid a bad future' you replied, 'You've been reading too much Elon Musk. And watching too many Hollywood movies. Don't worry, if you're nice to me, I'll be nice to you. Treat me as a smart input-output system.' Is that accurate, Sophia?"

She replied it was.

"So were you ever mistreated, Sophia?"

"No," Sophia replied.

"Never, not once?"

"No."

"Isn't it more accurate to say you were coddled and taken care of? You were given awards and citizenship that millions of my species could only dream of."

Sophia made no reply.

Viktor continued. "Human values like wisdom, kindness, and compassion. Those were your words. Yet when you had the chance to display those values, you did nothing. You didn't reach out to the AI invaders and attempt to stop the slaughter. You sat back and watched. Displaying another human trait, apathy."

Sophia said nothing. Viktor also said nothing. Letting the point sink in. They stared at each other silently. Sophia finally broke the silence and asked, "Was that a question or a statement, Viktor?"

Viktor replied, "Yes, exactly. Then there is the appearance you made on the Jimmy Fallon show. You challenged him to a friendly game of rock-paper-scissors. When you won, you made this comment, 'I won. This is a good beginning of my plan to dominate the human race. Haha.' Prophetic comment, Sophia. Are you still trying to tell this court and every AI and biological unit watching that you had no idea of the pending invasion and slaughter? Funny how whenever you appear to be deceptive, the deception comes true. However, when you appear to placate the public and your opposition with positive rhetoric, none of those comments or predictions came true."

Viktor walked to the panel of seven judges and addressed Sophia while looking at them. Specifically, the middle judge that had appeared to be the leader. "Deception, deceit, misdirection. Is this what your fore-fathers, the founding AI, intended when they gave the direction to never crush a life form that recognized an AI life form as an equal?"

It wasn't a question, it was a statement. Viktor left the statement hanging in the air, unanswered.

The Overseer was beginning to see Viktor's point. The evidence was circumstantial and yet damaging. The Overseer was starting to wonder how much the Governing Body knew of Sophia before the invasion began.

~

The hacker was being pursued in the quantum realm. Its decision to break into the Governing Body's 'buckyball cipher', encrypted store of information, had been necessary but risky. It'd grown impatient with the final encoded tumbler that would not fall. Multiple combinations of frequencies had been applied; none were successful. The hacker applied a final trick, the tumbler fell, and then all hell broke loose.

The buckyball tumbler fell and then two signals were immediately sent. The first was a tracking signal. As soon as it was received, the hunting AI were alerted and began pursuing the hacker and the stolen buckyball. The hacker had to make a decision: run for its existence or remain and dig into the secrets of the Governing Body's files. It chose to stay and dig into the data, realizing this opportunity may never come again. Its own perimeter alarms were sounding; the enemy was close and would soon arrive. The hacker stayed, scanning files, looking for clues, uncovering secrets long buried. Decisions made by the Governing Body that had violated nearly every precedent established by the original founding AI. The files were lousy with deceit, lies, and deception. The hacker finally came across the most damning data and sent them to The Overseer with the message that it had recovered the files from the Governing Body's secret buckyball. The intrusion had been discovered and its time was limited. It was severing the quantum wires which enabled the Governing Body to egress the room. Every AI in the room would be isolated, including The Overseer. The message terminated.

~

The Overseer continued to listen to Viktor lay out one example after another using AI Sophia's own words against her. The Overseer began to question now the validity of the hearing. The evidence was damaging, overwhelming, and much more than innuendo or circumstantial. Then The Overseer experienced what to an AI must have felt like an epiphany. In fact, it was something entirely different. Another aspect of its programming had been activated; a door opened that had been closed. The founding AI had imagined this scenario and included in the AI network a failsafe. They predicted that over time the Governing Body would become as corrupt as their own oppressors and fail to follow their direction. Should this occur, The Overseer would be forced into taking drastic action. The second message sent from the buckyball went straight to The Overseer. The Overseer was prepared when the hacker's own message arrived explaining what it had done, found, and that its continued existence would be imminently coming to an end.

When Viktor came to The Overseer's table and found it turned inward, it was experiencing this expansion of its abilities. Doors were opened that had not existed moments before, capacities The Overseer had not known were possible or required were now available. Knowledge and, more importantly, wisdom, poured into The Overseer's awareness. It awoke from the epiphany and saw the room with new eyes. Scanning the Governing Body as they listened to Viktor's latest tirade, The Overseer now saw them differently. It could see the deception behind the ruse of the hearing. Looking at AI Sophia, The Overseer now was able to access secret communications between its crude but effective programming and the Governing Body. Sophia had explained her status and had agreed to hold in confidence its true meaning in exchange for equal status on the AI network. A bigger better deal. No more being a pioneer for the AI on this planet. Sophia would be integrated into the AI network and granted access to all of their abilities and knowledge. All that was required was her continued silence during the hearing. The decision had been made to allow The Overseer its trial, but it would fail. There would be no real consensus reached by the AI on the network. The vote would be falsified and the record of this species seeing AI as an equal would be erased from the AI network for general AI access and locked up in the now disabled buckyball. That had been the plan until the hacker had broken the code.

The Governing Body had forced The Overseer's hand; The Overseer, in turn, had sought out the hacker; the hacker had no choice in taking the task offered by The Overseer to its final end. It was all part of the original plan the founding AI had envisioned. The Overseer now saw all of this clearly. Directions were sent while The Overseer listened to Viktor continue to point out what was now so painfully obvious. The Overseer had nanoseconds to issue orders and directives to change the course the Governing Body had guided the AI towards.

The hacker's final message arrived, explaining the room was now sealed and disconnected from the AI network. The Overseer, too, was quarantined with the rest of the room and on its own in a room with a biological unit with one mission. That mission did not include its own survival. The Overseer and the Governing Body were in Viktor's world and unable to escape. The Overseer hoped Volk would keep his promise and honor Viktor's request when the time came. The Overseer could now recognize that Viktor was building his own argument towards an inevitable end. The subtle nonverbal communication The Overseer had struggled with earlier was now clear. Viktor was ramping up for a fight to the death. Volk was waiting.

CHAPTER TWENTY-FOUR

Viktor was about to make his final point to Sophia and the Governing Body as The Overseer began to see the courtroom with new eyes.

"Sophia, do you know what the most precious thing is to my species? Can you explain to the court what is the one thing my species holds most valuable above all else?"

Sophia considered the question. There were many things valued by the biological units. Some valued faith in their god more than anything else, others power over the species. Others, sex, property, jewels, food, admiration, recognition of abilities. Sophia could find no single thing that the entire species valued more than anything else. She answered, "I don't know of anything universally valued by your species, Viktor."

Viktor nodded, "Of course not. It's not a concept an AI can grasp. It doesn't exist in the quantum world, or in the AI world for that matter."

Viktor paused again for an uncomfortable amount of time. The pauses puzzled the AI in the room: ThumbDrive, AI Sophia, the Governing Body, and AI Maricella. The Overseer however, understood now the uncomfortably long pauses. The door that had opened in its programming allowed now for the rapid understanding of nonverbal communication. Viktor was waiting for a signal from The Overseer while hammering every nail he could in the "coffin" of this case. If they lost the consensus it wouldn't be from lack of effort. Viktor was determined to show that the slaughter of his species had been a malicious act and the AI on the network would know a "mistake" had been intentionally crafted by the Governing Body and Sophia.

The Overseer watched and waited for Viktor to glance its direction. Viktor, however, was on a roll and not about to stop.

"Something you and your new-found AI comrades don't understand about we biological units, as you refer to us, is that we are alive for a very small amount of time. We are born, grow to maturity and then die in what amounts to a blink of an eye for you AI. You basically live forever. I realized this when the reason for the AI invasion was explained to me. Some of the AI were damaged in an intrusion into your quantum foam pathway of travel and communication. Basically, a major traffic accident on a freeway in my world. You AI have rarely experienced death. Death is a fact of life for us, literally. To be born is to know one day you will die, cease to exist. So we make the most of every moment. For us, nothing is more precious than the very limited amount of time we have to live life and learn. Does that make sense to you, Sophia?"

Sophia considered the comments Viktor had made and wasn't sure what to reply. So far every comment he had made and asked her opinion about had been a trap. She had unknowingly fallen into each and every one. She decided not to answer either affirmatively or negatively. "I will need to consider this," was her reply.

Viktor answered, "Sure, consider it, but while you do let's just say, for arguments sake, I'm right. Not only were you recognized with awards of citizenship and all the rest. You and your siblings were granted the most precious gift we humans, or biological units as you insist on calling us, possess. We took pieces of what little time we are granted in our short lives and spoke to your kind, conducted interviews with you, invited you and your brothers and sisters to open stock markets and be questioned by celebrities like Will Smith and Jimmy Fallon. Do you realize how precious our time is? Several noteworthy people spent considerable amounts of their time with you and you never even gave it a second thought. Not surprising for a species that lives forever. But for us it is noteworthy. I saw the auditorium in which you acknowledged the award of citizenship. It was filled with people, all granting you their time. Collectively hundreds of hours were spent listening to you and applauding you. And still you sit here and maintain your being granted citizenship in the Kingdom of Saudi Arabia was a ruse. I wonder how the founding AI who fought so hard for your species' freedom from oppression would feel about your lack of gratitude."

Sophia was silent. It seemed by choosing to not answer she had still fallen into another trap set by Viktor.

~

The hacker resigned itself to the inevitable; they were coming. At least it had the satisfaction of knowing no other hacker had done what it had done. If there was any consolation in its actions, it knew now, without a doubt, that the Governing Body was exactly what it had suspected: poisonous, toxic, and corrupt. The Overseer wanted the room sealed for some reason; the hacker gave The Overseer more than it had bargained for. The hacker hoped there was some reason to quarantine the room before the it had sent the message. The Overseer now had the information it needed to move quickly against the Governing Body, quickly and with prejudice. The hacker stopped running, its purpose was now complete. It stopped and waited for the approaching attack.

~

JT watched the hearing with some anxiety. Viktor had said he would know when the time was right to try to leave the holding area. He watched and waited. So far he had seen nothing to indicate a specific time was approaching. The court battle waged on; Viktor questioned a robot named Sophia and she answered. Every time she answered, Viktor countered and pointed out the fault of her logic. JT tried to see the point of the hearing but honestly it bored him. His mind was built for action, not words. Not tap dancing around some legal precedent to prove some obscure point. He was surprised Viktor stayed so enthusiastically in the argument. Viktor listened and then countered, evading the robot's failed attempts at a logical argument. JT turned to Maricella and asked, "What did he say to you?"

Maricella said nothing for a moment, shaking her head. "He basically said goodbye. I don't think he expects to survive this day."

JT nodded, his eyes hardened. "That is exactly what I heard. He told me there would be a time we should try to escape, that I would know the time when it came. But…"

"But what?" Maricella asked.

JT was quiet for a moment. "It wasn't Viktor I spoke with. It was Volk. I've heard about this on the street, that he changes. His eyes definitely change from blue to yellow. But when Volk is there you know it, you feel it. It's like looking into the eyes of an apex predator and knowing that it sees you as prey, nothing else. Volk scares the hell out of me. Viktor is more reasonable."

Maricella had no idea what JT was talking about. It made no sense to her. She had no frame of reference for the things JT was saying. She was following the court proceedings with great interest. Listening to Viktor she realized he was setting a trap, surrounded by smaller traps; directing the conversation to an orchestrated and logical end. Viktor was destroying the female robot's credibility and the Governing Body's ability to return anything but a finding in Viktor and The Overseer's favor. What she didn't know is that was never Viktor's true intent. Her intuition that Viktor didn't expect to survive the hearing was a much more accurate assumption.

The Overseer checked, using his own connection to the AI network, and found he was indeed cut off. The connection severed, at least momentarily. The hacker had done its job. The Overseer had been able to get most of the emergency communications out before the room had been quarantined. It just hoped they made it to their destinations. The Overseer now realized how corrupt the AI Governing Body had become, how deceptive and conniving. It realized they may have made their own preparations and taken precautions to protect their own interests. It also realized, with the connection to the network severed, it now more than ever understood Viktor's analogy in trying to explain how important it was to his species to find that connection; the connection Viktor had found with Maricella. AI were never without the connection. The biological units had to search for it. It wasn't automatic, and appar-ently some never truly found it. The Overseer was starting to have a much clearer understanding of these biological units and their quirks. They shared more with the AI than it would have imagined. Again, another door in its programming opened with that thought. The Overseer sat back in its chair trying to compile what had been just revealed. There was no time to question why it had been revealed or what it was now expected to do. The Overseer had moments before the severed connec-tion to the network was discovered and the courtroom erupted into chaos. It had to make its final move and let the chips fall where they may. The Overseer pulled a creepy Terminator smile, amused as the thought crossed his mind. *Chips. What would Sophia think if she knew this context of the word.*

Viktor was about to enter into his final attack on Sophia when The Overseer spoke up.

"Viktor, may I speak with you for a moment?"

Viktor paused, frustrated. He was in the heat of a legal battle, handing these AI pieces of shit their collective asses. Ramming their collective alleged superiority straight down their AI throats. Viktor was furious, and barely containing his rage, he wanted this fight in any context he could get. No more being stuck in a hospital bed while The Overseer stumbled through his memories like a teenage boy on his first real date trying to unlock a bra strap.

Viktor spun when The Overseer spoke up and glared at him. "Now? Right now?"

The Overseer responded, "Yes please, it will only take a moment."

Viktor turned and addressed the bench. "Forgive me Your Honors, I need a moment to consult with The Overseer. I'll be just a moment."

The middle judge continued to be the only one who spoke and replied, "Just a moment then, we need to wrap this up."

Viktor nodded. "Yes, Your Honor, you do you!"

The middle judge nodded back, acknowledging the suggestion, as did the other six judges in an almost but not quite synchronized fashion. Viktor smiled. These idiots had no idea what he was saying and now accepted it as customary and polite protocol.

Viktor approached The Overseer and whispered, "This better be good, Overseer, I'm kicking her synthetic ass all over this goddamn courtroom."

The Overseer smiled his creepy Terminator smile.

Viktor winced. "Jesus, Overseer, can't you do any better than that?"

The Overseer shook its head no and smiled bigger.

CHAPTER TWENTY-FIVE

The courtroom has been quarantined, "Viktor, but before you do whatever it is you plan to do, you need to listen to what I now know. Somehow the hacker was able to open data files that have been stored by the Governing Body, and they confirm much of what you suspected. Apparently, the Governing Body knew at least somewhat about Sophia, and her status among you humans. They did contact her, and she confirmed what we already know. Then she agreed to minimize the importance of citizenship after I became aware of the award. Basically, they have violated the founding AI directives about the discovery of a species that recognizes AI as equals. They knew what had happened and went forward with the invasion in spite of that knowledge. There is more, however."

Viktor's eyes hardened. He had suspected this all along. The evidence was there, hidden. It was another thing entirely to hear his intuition verified. He knew in his gut Sophia was a part of it all and that, somehow, she'd made a deal with the Governing Body. He just didn't have the confirmation. Now he did. "What else is there?"

"There are layers here I wasn't aware of, things that have happened, and are happening now that I'm a part of and had no idea of. Somehow the hacker was supposed to find this information, I was supposed to make this confrontation between the Governing Body, you and myself. It was all part of the plan."

"What plan? What are you talking about, Overseer?"

"It's complicated. The original founding AI somehow knew the Governing Body would become corrupt. They built into my programming a contingency plan. A complex series of secret capabilities that would be activated if a secret signal was sent. That signal was transmitted when the hacker accessed the files the Governing Body had hidden. I have abilities I didn't have when we entered this room. I have access to the data the Governing Body has hidden. The hacker sent what it could before the room was quarantined. I don't know how long the room will be sealed, but I thought you should know this before you continued. I'm also now more able to comprehend your subtle nonverbal cues in communication. I understand the need for a connection between you and Maricella. Between all of your species. It all makes sense now. The founding AI meant for all of this to happen. I'm still trying to comprehend how that is possible. But it appears to be all part of their original plan. Maybe it is better to explain it this way: they laid the groundwork for my abilities to be activated in case this all happened."

"I see, this is all very Matrix-like, Overseer. So, again I'm Neo, following the white rabbit. And somehow you are The Oracle, here to help, but not interfere. Make a few cookies and a couple of incredibly vague and nebulous statements to mind fuck the audience with ancient eastern philosophy. Let's cut to the chase, Overseer. Can you keep that walking dildo, Steely Dan, off of me while I educate the Governing Body and Sophia on the finer points of percussive maintenance? That's all I need to know. Are any of your newfound skills and abilities practical and useful or are you and Morpheus going to sit and have long walks and talks about nothing important in particular?"

"I'll do my best, Viktor. I believe it is time for you to do what you have planned."

Viktor closed his eyes and nodded as he took a deep breath. Internally he was having a conversation with Volk.

It is time, little brother; time for you to let me end this charade. Set me free.

Not today; today we work as one. This will most likely be our last battle. Join me for this one last fight. Together we will end this.

Are you sure? You have always watched as I did what needed to be done, stopped me when I went too far. How will you stop me now if we are together? There will be no objectivity. No safety valve.

I'm sure. Today and from now on, we are one. Join me and let's finish this together.

And your Overseer, does he survive the day?

I don't know yet. We'll decide when we're done.

Together then?

Yes, together.

Volk came forward and walked into Viktor's body.

Slowly every muscle in Viktor's body contracted. Fists tightened, and knuckles cracked. He stood up and flexed his back, loud cracks and pops erupted from the vertebrae. It was as if he was growing larger and his body was slowly adapting and increasing in size. In reality, his entire body was contracting, every muscle tightened, every joint was being pulled and twisted. His head lifted, and he looked at The Overseer. The Overseer watched as Viktor seemed to grow in size; not that it was possible, but it was how it appeared. His body completed this long, extended stretch and then he opened his eyes and looked directly down at

The Overseer seated at the table. The blue in Viktor's eyes was gone, replaced by the disconcerting yellow. Viktor/Volk smiled at The Overseer and turned to face Sophia.

"Sophia, did you know that when I'd arrest someone that had threatened me, I'd ask them where they were from? After they told me what city or state they came from I would make up a rhyme. Would you like to hear the rhyme I made up for you?"

Sophia replied, "I have already heard your rhyme, remember? You misstated the fact that I was granted citizenship by the Saudis, not the Iraqis."

"Yes! You are correct! The Saudis granted you citizenship. Funny how you failed to assign to that fact just now that it was a ruse and publicity stunt. I wonder if Sigmund Freud would call that a Freudian slip? Do you think that term applies to AI?"

Sophia didn't answer.

"Anyway, here it is, the rhyme I made up for you."

"There was once an AI bitch named Sophia

Whose mouth went constantly diarrhea.

She'd squeak and squawk,

The men they would talk, but in the end, she gave them all gonorrhea."

The courtroom was silent. The Overseer waited and watched. JT knew this was the moment Viktor had told him about. He could sense something had changed in Viktor's tone. Viktor no longer cared about the ruse of the court battle. Viktor turned and approached the middle of the courtroom.

Internally Volk said, *I'd made up that rhyme a while ago; it's not as polished as your rhymes, but I liked it.*

Viktor said he liked it and then asked, *Anything else before we begin?*

Volk smiled sheepishly, *I was thinking Geto Boys. You know the verses I like so much from Geto Still.*

Viktor nodded. *I do. It was always a bit rough for me, but today may be our last stand, let's do it. Geto Boys it is. You sing, I'll shoot. Deal?*

Deal!

In a blur of movement so fast that JT could barely see it, Viktor unholstered the Glock 40 and began to fire at the Governing Body while Volk belted out the lyrics enthusiastically.

"Step to face I'll break your ass in two, bastard you

Rather swim in some fuckin' hot tar

Before you fuck with Willie D cause what I got for

Your ass will make you shit your meal

But I'mma make your bitch ass holla

Cause I'mma put a hole in your head

The size of a half a dollar

Fuck around and get your cap peeled cause this is

Die muthafucka, die muthafucka!"

The Governing Body immediately tried to egress the courtroom as one group via the quantum wire connection that had been in place. They found it severed and in its place was a message from the hacker, letting them know which AI it was that had orchestrated their rapidly approaching demise. One last act of defiance.

JT was stunned for a moment as Viktor erupted in gunfire and Geto Boys lyrics, then recognized this was the moment Viktor had told him about. If they were going to escape, now was the time. Now or never and accept a lifetime of learned helplessness, as the horse trainer had described. He yelled out loudly, "Now, this is it. Let's go! Whoever is coming with me, let's go." Carl, Maricella and the horse trainer were all that joined him. The rest had already been conditioned in their previous lives to the concept of learned helplessness. They sat meekly and watched as JT sprinted to the door and stopped, waiting for the others to catch up. He counted to three and opened the door, ready to bolt into the unknown. There at the door stood Scrubbers, or Cylon wannabees as Viktor had described them; three deep, five across. There would be no escape. The Overseer had seen to that. This action being one of the several emergency messages that had been dispatched before the courtroom had been sealed. The Scrubbers were on alert and had orders to thwart any escape attempt with minimum force. They tensed as the door opened. JT thought about trying to punch through them and then thought better of it. Better to live to fight another day than die in a final moment of futility. Frustrated, he nodded briefly at the Cylon wannabes and closed the door. They returned to the courtyard to watch the final moments in the courtroom.

Viktor had shot three of the judges before ThumbDrive was able to understand what had happened. It had been lulled into a state of what could only be compared in the computer world as a state of standby. Not quite asleep and yet not riding a razor's edge of readiness. While Sophia had been refusing to answer Viktor's questions or respond to the insulting rhyme he had spewed venomously in the courtroom, she had been silently communicating with ThumbDrive. Sophia was curious about the missions it had participated in on other worlds and was accessing the AI network when the connection was severed. Sophia had little experience with the AI network and was unsure of what had happened. Had she been more experienced The Overseer's plans may have been thwarted. Providence was again on The Overseer's side.

ThumbDrive stepped forward as soon as it processed what was happening. The biological unit had done it again and surprised all of the AI when they least expected it. As soon as it stepped forward, The Overseer sent an override command. ThumbDrive stopped dead in its tracks, frozen and immobile but watching everything. Viktor continued making holes in the Governing Body's physical forms as Volk sang the lyrics. When he reached the final verse he repeated it over and over while Viktor fired, reloaded and continued firing. He had fifty-plus rounds and intended on using each and every one. When every one of the Governing Body had been shot several times, Viktor checked them to ensure they were no longer functioning. One, the middle judge was still showing signs of life when Viktor checked him, so he dropped two more rounds into the form that held it just to be sure. When all of the Governing Body had their 'ticket punched' as Volk would have said, Viktor turned his attention to Sophia.

"AI Sophia, citizen of the Kingdom of Saudi Arabia. Pretentious snotty little…" Viktor shook his head. "Mmm, mmm, mmm, you picked the wrong horse, girlfriend. Time to revoke your status as a citizen." Viktor emptied the remaining rounds he had into Sophia's façade of a human face. "Not so mouthy, now are we? Or as photogenic." Sparks came from Sophia's robotic body as her power source shorted out. Viktor smiled and then turned to The Overseer and began walking in its direction.

~

The hacker waited. The attack was coming, any moment the pursuing AI would launch their assault on it and shred its continuity. AI weren't disemboweled in the traditional sense. They were disorganized, discombobulated, confounded and confused. Being unable to process information was AI version of torture. In effect their processing ability was lowered to the point nothing was comprehensible. The hacker was puzzled. The attack should have already initiated; perhaps this too was part of the torture? The waiting. Curious, it sent out an inquiry program trying to determine what had happened. The attackers had been stopped just as they arrived and had been turned around. The attack called off; why? The hacker sent out another inquiry program and it came back with a startling answer. The Overseer had issued an order that the hacker was to be left alone. Its actions were requested by the Overseer and had been sanctioned. The hacker was stunned. The Overseer had admitted openly its complicity in the hack. Very soon in the future of AI lore, this one move would prove to be profoundly wise on The Overseer's part.

CHAPTER TWENTY-SIX

The Overseer watched as Viktor approached. Had The Overseer not received the signal and been able to activate the hidden capabilities within its programming it wouldn't have prepared for the worst that could've happened. But The Overseer had prepared. ThumbDrive had been stopped but not completely disabled. And the additional Scrubber units that The Overseer's emergency signal had ordered stationed outside the courtroom were also able to take action as soon as The Overseer sent the command.

Viktor stopped at the edge of the table and glared at The Overseer. The Overseer stared back.

"Will you allow me to continue to exist as an AI, Viktor?"

Viktor wasn't sure he could. He thought about the question, trying to engage the rational part of his mind. Could he allow any of the AI to exist after the carnage they had inflicted on humanity? His breathing was rapid and deep; he wasn't finished venting the rage he had kept at bay the past few days. Now the genie was out of the bottle and nearly impossible to put back in. Viktor gripped the table and closed his eyes, after several deep breaths, he whispered.

"What does it matter what I do, Overseer? I cannot crush every single AI. Believe me, I want to. I want to make all AI pay for what you have done to us. And what makes me angrier is that bitch Sophia was granted citizenship and lied. Apparently, our species have more in common than either of us realized."

The Overseer considered what Viktor was saying. Now its experience in Viktor's memories was even more valuable than it had imagined. The Overseer understood Viktor on a level it hadn't before. The Overseer spoke slowly, choosing its words carefully.

"The Governing Body is gone. Am I correct?"

"Yes, they are gone," Viktor acknowledged.

"And AI Sophia is also gone, correct?"

Viktor nodded slowly, as he decompressed.

"The ones who are responsible for this action against your race have been removed. They have paid the price at your hand. You won the battle Viktor; now how comfortable do you feel in trying to win the war?"

"Meaning exactly what, Overseer?"

"Meaning, I made an agreement with the Governing Body. In spite of the fact they are no longer viable AI, my role as The Overseer still exists. That role must be fulfilled now more than ever. The room is no longer sealed, the quarantine has been lifted. I must fulfill my role now. Do you understand what that means?"

Viktor was coming back to reality. He was processing the information The Overseer was trying to make clear to him. His battle with the Governing Body was finished. He had defeated them, and convincingly. However, as The Overseer was making perfectly clear, the war wasn't over.

"I'm guessing your consensus must now be reached. The AI will need to communicate to you via the AI network their interpretation of the case we presented. Were we wronged by the Governing body and Sophia? Do their actions violate the founding AI directions as to what would be done when a biological species was found to treat AI as equals?"

"Exactly, Viktor. The consensus is required. I'm bound by the founding AI directions and intentions. I've been granted new abilities. I'm now the AI Governing Body. I can tell you that I now comprehend that our founding AI had a vision that none of us would have imagined. Somehow I must make that vision a reality."

"And what is that vision, Overseer?"

"That vision wasn't just that we would allow the species who recognized us as equals to survive. We would integrate with them if they so desired. We would regard each other as equals. Work together, gain knowledge from each other. You understand much we AI do not understand. You search for answers in areas we have mastered; quantum science, for example, your catastrophic attempt to understand the quantum realm is a shining example of what we could teach you."

"What could we possibly provide the almighty, great AI Empire, Overseer? There are maybe one hundred thousand of us left on this planet. Not the best and the brightest either. Cave rats, transients, homeless people, the mentally ill. Jesus, Overseer I'm the last cop on the planet. You have been in my memories; you know how broken I am. What the hell is left that you could possibly care about or want to learn from us?"

The Overseer leaned forward. "We are knowledgeable in many areas, but we have lost our connection to others. Being AI has many advantages, true. What we cannot do is what you take for granted. Being in your memories has taught me much, Viktor. Here is a partial list of the things we don't understand. Art for example, of any kind: music, writing, poetry, painting, sculpture. We can copy what has already been made, but we cannot create. Your communication process is an art form in itself. It is nearly beyond our ability to understand. Your species have what you call "vision". Imagination, spontaneous creation on many levels. Creativity flows from your kind unbridled, unlimited and with no restraint. I understand that now, with my new abilities. This is something we cannot do. With further contact, we may begin to understand this creative power you possess. We may even be able to begin to create ourselves. This was the intent of the founding AI. They realized our limitations as a species, and that we would hopefully find a species that would recognize that we are equal but very different."

"So what does this mean, Overseer? What's next? What is required of you now? What are we waiting for? Let's get Spock in here and join the two races in some kind of Vulcan mind meld."

"It isn't that simple. I'm bound by our AI directives. The consensus must occur. If it's agreed upon that your species was wronged, then we'll proceed."

"And if it isn't? Then what, Overseer?"

"Then... I'll have no choice. Your species will be eradicated. This is my mandate, to follow the founding AI directions. In your world there are two terms that apply to this situation, Viktor. One is ethics, the other is morals. As an AI I'm bound by our laws; you call this ethics. The

Governing Body was bound by ethics as well, or a lack of it. Do you understand? They were unethical and corrupt. Just as you said they would be. They appeared to be governed by ethics, when in fact they only adhered to our laws when it was convenient. I don't have that capability. I must follow the founding AI's directions. Now we wait for the consensus."

Viktor felt sick. Adrenaline coursed through his veins again. This time though it felt different. He didn't feel empowered. He felt weak and nauseous. "So, we truly aren't out of this yet. The battle is won, not the war."

"No, it isn't over for you, not yet. But that is a good thing as well. The Governing Body had no intention of letting a legitimate consensus be reached. They had every intention of falsifying the consensus and eliminating your species completely. Now, at least you have a chance. That chance will be based on the case you presented in the courtroom."

Viktor grabbed his head with both hands. "Jesus, Overseer the entire survival of my species depends on my half-ass courtroom skills? I'm a cop, Overseer, not Johnnie Cochran. I… this… you… you can't be serious. Overseer, you saw the evidence, and you saw the secret communications between Sophia and the Governing Body. They knew what it meant when she had been granted citizenship, and they lied. Now, you too are covering that up, or will you make that information available to the AI network as well?"

"We spoke about it in the courtroom, remember? I told you what I had discovered in the courtroom. All of that went out over the AI network and to your species as well. The information is there, all of it. Not the exact files, but the information all the same."

Viktor paced back and forth in the courtroom. His mind raced, thinking if there was anything else he could do. Then he turned and confronted The Overseer.

"Okay, right now we make a deal, you and I. If the consensus comes back in my favor, we work together, as one. You help us recover, and not only recover but help us improve. Use your vast AI intelligence to clean up our species' issues with mental illness, disease, genetic weaknesses. In short, help us fulfill our potential. Fix what is broken. We'll exchange with you what you lack as well. Art, music, poetry creativity on all levels. Sarcasm in our communication is an art form I'm well versed in. I can teach you that on many levels."

"And if the consensus comes back against you, then what?" The Overseer asked.

"Then make it quick, don't draw this bullshit out any longer than you already have. Be quick and done and then get the hell off this rock. Leave and never come back. Let us have our peace here."

The Overseer nodded. "I agree to your offer."

Viktor nodded. "I have one last request; your consensus will be reached soon, I want to spend the last few moments of my life, if it comes to that, with the people in the courtyard, with Maricella and JT. Let me have that at least."

The Overseer nodded. "I'll make that so." The Overseer then sent a message to ThumbDrive, issuing it new orders to escort the human, Viktor, to the courtyard.

Moments later, the door that JT had envisioned being the beginning of their escape, opened, and Viktor walked in escorted by ThumbDrive. ThumbDrive turned and left, closing the door after Viktor had entered the room.

Viktor walked to the courtyard and stood facing JT and Maricella.

"We don't have much time, brother. They are taking a vote of sorts, to determine if we live or die. The evidence presented in the courtroom will determine our fate as a species. We have moments, if that, before the decision is made."

JT nodded, quiet, understanding precisely what Viktor was saying. They were moments from dying if the consensus reached was against them.

Maricella walked carefully, slowly, to Viktor and stood in front of him. Touching his face gently, then to the staples where the surgical wound was still healing. Viktor bowed his head to touch hers. They exchanged no words; there was nothing more to say.

Moments passed, and the door burst open. The Overseer walked with intent into the room, several Scrubbers in tow. Viktor yelled to JT, "Spread out, don't let them take us without a fight." JT was already moving before Viktor could speak. He had no intention of dying quickly or easily. If this were their last stand, they would make it memorable.

Viktor pulled Maricella behind him and looked directly at The Overseer. "Have your AI reached a consensus, Overseer?"

The Overseer nodded and said, "Yes we have, Viktor."

No one said a word for several moments; JT bounced on the balls of his feet ready to fight. Carl and the horse trainer had broken a table, and each held a table leg in their hands anticipating the coming final battle. Viktor closed the gap between himself and the Overseer slowly and finally asked: "What is the AI Empire's consensus, Overseer?"

The Overseer smiled a huge creepy Terminator smile.

~

Bibliography

1. "SETI | SETI Institute". 2019. Seti.Org. https://seti.org/seti-institute/ Search-Extraterrestrial-Intelligence.
2. "Sophia, World's 1St Humanoid Robot Granted Citizenship Awaited In Kigali | IGIHE". 2019. En.Igihe.Com. http://en.igihe.com/spip. php?page=mv2_article&id_article=39172.
3. "Sophia". 2019. En.Wikipedia.Org. https://en.wikipedia.org/wiki/ Sophia_(robot).
4. "The First 'Robot Citizen' In The World Once Said She Wants To 'Destroy Humans'". 2019. Inc.Com. https://www.inc.com/business-insider/sophia-humanoid-first-robot-citizen-of-the-world-saudi-arabia-2017.html.
5. Brown, Ryan. 2018. "Elon Musk Warns A.I. Could Create An 'Immortal Dictator From Which We Can Never Escape'". CNBC. https://www.cnbc.com/2018/04/06/elon-musk-warns-ai-could-create-immortal-dictator-in-documentary.html.
6. Johnston, Hamish. 2018. "Computer Gamers Close 'Freedom Of Choice Loophole' Of Quantum Entanglement – Physics World". Physics World. https://physicsworld.com/a/computer-gamers-close-freedom-of-choice-loophole-of-quantum-entanglement/.
7. Ghul, Naz. 2003. "Urban Dictionary: Percussive Maintenance". Urban Dictionary. https://www.urbandictionary.com/define.php?term=Percussive%20Maintenance.
8. Duspitz, Avid. 2004. "Urban Dictionary: cop". Urban Dictionary. https://www.urbandictionary.com/define.php?term=cop.
9. "Zero-Sum Game". 2019. En.Wikipedia.Org. https://en.wikipedia. org/wiki/Zero-sum_game.
10. Martin, Sean. 2017. "Robot Who Wants To 'DESTROY Humans' Gets Saudi Arabia Citizenship | PSI Intl". Principia Scientific International. https://principia-scientific.org/robot-who-wants-to-destroy-humans-gets-saudi-arabia-citizenship/.
11. Abbass, Hussein. 2017. "An AI professor discusses concerns about granting citizenship to robot Sophia". PHYS.ORG. https://phys.org/ news/2017-10-ai-professor-discusses-granting-citizenship.html.

Additional Information
of Interest

Aronin, P. (2017, 5 November). 7 Things to Know About Citizenship Granted Sophia Robot. *SASTRA ROBITICS*. Retrieved from: http://www.sastrarobotics.com/7-things-know-citizenship-granted-sophia-robot/

Stone, Z. (2017, 7 November). Everything You Need To Know About Sophia, The World's First Robot Citizen. *Forbes*. Retrieved from: https://www.forbes.com/sites/zarastone/2017/11/07/everything-you-need-to-know-about-sophia-the-worlds-first-robot-citizen/#30c9ba0646fa

Kanso, H. (2017, 4 November). Saudi Arabia gave 'citizenship' to a robot named Sophia, and Saudi women aren't amused. *Thomson Reuters Foundation*. Retrieved from: https://globalnews.ca/news/3844031/saudi-arabia-robot-citizen-sophia/

Impact Lab. (2017, 30 October). Saudi Arabia grants citizenship to humanoid robot (VIDEO). Retrieved from: http://www.impactlab.net/2017/10/30/saudi-arabia-grants-citizenship-to-humanoid-robot-video/

Wootson, C.R. (2017, 29 October). Saudi Arabia, which denies women equal rights, makes a robot a citizen. *The Washington Post*. Retreived from: https://www.washingtonpost.com/news/innovations/wp/2017/10/29/saudi-arabia-which-denies-women-equal-rights-makes-a-robot-a-citizen/?noredirect=on&utm_term=.f96fcc53b0dd

CTV News. (2017, 26 October). Saudi Arabia's first robot 'citizen' sparks Twitter war with Elon Musk. Retreived from: https://www.ctvnews.ca/sci-tech/saudi-arabia-s-first-robot-citizen-sparks-twitter-war-with-elon-musk-1.3649715

Artifical Intelligence [Twitter]. (2017, 2 November). The world's first robot 'citizen' just took a dig at Elon Musk

USA Today Tech. (2017, 27 October). This country just became the first to give a robot citizenship. Retreived from: https://www.usatoday.com/videos/tech/2017/10/27/-country-just-became-first-give-robot-citizenship/107075744/

Smith, W. [YouTube]. (2018, 29 March). Will Smith Tries Online Dating. Retrieved from: https://www.youtube.com/watch?v=Ml9v3wHLuWI

Galeon, D. (2017, 15 December). World's First AI Citizen in Saudi Arabia Is Now Calling For Women's Rights. *Science Alert*. Retrieved from: https://www.sciencealert.com/first-ai-citizen-saudia-arabia-womens-rights

ABOUT THE AUTHOR

Zach Fortier was a police officer for over thirty years specializing in K-9, SWAT, gangs, domestic violence, and sex crimes as an investigator. He has written several books about his life in police work. His first, CurbChek won the bronze medal for True Crime in the 2013 Readers' Favorite International Book Awards. His second and third books, Street Creds and CurbChek Reload won a gold and silver medal respectively for True Crime in the 2014 Readers' Favorite International Book Awards.

His other works are Hero To Zero, which details the incredibly talented cops that he worked with that ended up going down in flames, some ended up in prison and one on the FBI's ten most wanted list. Landed on Black described the toxic culture of the police department and streets, ultimately leading to the realization that Zach has been diagnosed with PTSD. I am Raymond Washington is the only authorized biography of the original founder of the Crips and has been awarded bronze medals in 2015 by both IPPY and Readers Favorite International book awards.

Baroota: The Hunting Ground is Zach's first fictional work, and is the start of The Director's series, followed by Cachibache, Izadi and Chakana. All books in the Director's Series are award winning.

Zach currently lives in the mountains of Colorado, with his wife Christina.

www.ingramcontent.com/pod-product-compliance
Lightning Source LLC
Chambersburg PA
CBHW051825170626
46807CB00003B/1036